Guided Hearts

by

C. Ellen Culverwell

Guided Hearts

Cover Art by *The Wild Rose Press, Inc.*

The Wild Rose Press, Inc.
PO Box 708
Adams Basin, NY 14410-0708
Visit us at www.thewildrosepress.com

Publishing History
First Edition, 2023
Trade Paperback ISBN 978-1-5092-4811-7
Digital ISBN 978-1-5092-4812-4

Published in the United States of America

The old woman asked, "Is there something I can do for you?"

"No, as usual I feel foolish. I'll gather myself together in a couple of minutes. My car is just over there," she said, pointing to the nearby cement path.

With a smirk, the woman said, "You know there is a cute young doctor who jogs through here every day. I know for a fact he's single. Maybe you could flag him down."

"Pick up a man in a cemetery? For all you know, I might be married with six kids."

Cocking her head to one side the woman replied, "Then the last place you'd be first thing in the morning is a cemetery."

Despite the circumstances Laurel found herself enjoying this odd woman. "You are."

"I'm old and have no life."

"In any event, thank you for your concern, but I'll be fine."

"Okay, I'll leave you to your headache."

Laurel watched the woman walk toward the development before placing her head in her hands to try to hold off on the urge to vomit. When she felt steady she stood to walk in the direction of her car. Just as she reached the path a jogger passed by.

Stopping, then turning, he gestured at her face. "What happened to you?"

"Do you want the long story or the short one?"

"I guess the short one."

"Stupidity."

He grinned. "That's generally the reason."

"Don't tell me you're a doctor."

His eyes widened. "How did you know?"

Dedication

For Hayley

Chapter One

As bank president, Laurel Tanner, the only woman and youngest person to hold that position, slid her key into the lock of the front door of the Bridgefield Bank. Admittedly she was there early but she believed in setting an example by being the first to arrive and the last to leave at the end of each day. Experience had taught her the employees respected her dedication and it was reciprocated. When the key refused to turn in the lock, she removed it. Perhaps she'd pulled the wrong one from her purse? She tried again with the same result and started to head for the back door to try that lock when a shadowed figure moved behind the closed blinds.

Heart racing with panic, she reached for her cellphone to call the police when a stranger opened the door. She took several steps backward not certain if she should run or stay.

"Mrs. Tanner?" the unfamiliar man asked.

Before she could answer, a second agent moved to tape a note to the front door of the bank. *TEMPORARILY CLOSED, SORRY FOR THE INCONVENIENCE.*

Outraged, she said, "You can't just close this bank without notice. I have employees and customers coming in to conduct business."

The agent, clearly unmoved, replied, "I can, and I

did. Now, where is your husband?"

Starting to feel lightheaded, she heard an odd buzzing sound in her ears. Suddenly she couldn't catch her breath. Why would federal agents ask about her husband? To keep from falling to the floor she quickly sank to a bench typically used by customers. Chaz is in Chicago on business."

"Are you certain of that?"

Laurel did not like the direction his questions were heading. "I am not answering any more questions until I know exactly what is happening here."

He handed her several documents. "In due time."

She examined the pages with the words *search and seizure* prominently displayed at the top. It still didn't answer any of the questions topmost on her mind.

The agent said, "This gives us complete access to examine all your bank records and to search your home."

"My home?" she said, raising her voice.

His cellphone rang, he instructed the caller to take all the computers and files.

By now, Laurel was practically breathless. "You have agents in my home? They are taking my personal possessions?"

He replied with an insidious smile. "We will, of course, give you an itemized receipt."

She had gleaned enough from their interactions so far to surmise her husband was in big trouble and the Feds considered her an accomplice. She tried to hold herself together, but feared she was going to become ill. She took deep breaths to compose herself. "I am the president of this bank and demand you give me some answers."

"You may demand anything you like, but that doesn't mean it will get you anywhere," the agent said, seeming to enjoy her discomfort.

She took out her cellphone and desperately tried to reach her husband. Chaz was the only one who could give her any answers. Her call went directly to voicemail.

"He is not going to answer, Mrs. Tanner. Unfortunately, he was one step ahead of us."

"Ahead of you on what? Please, I need to know."

In a matter-of-fact tone he replied, "I have a warrant for his arrest."

"Arrest?" she nearly shouted. "You can't be serious."

"Very serious."

"What are the charges?" she asked, fluctuating between anger and despair.

"He's been a very, very bad boy."

Laurel was not an imprudent person. Normally she weighed her options and thought before speaking but the agent was deliberately provoking a response. "I don't appreciate your sarcasm and condescending manner. If my husband has done something illegal, and that's a big if, what does it have to do with me and this bank?"

He smiled. "I need to know if your name needs to be added to the arrest warrant."

It took every ounce of self-control to keep her from slapping him. She'd never been treated with such disrespect and contempt. She was a kind and thoughtful person, finding herself in such a position was foreign to everything in her life. Her employees appreciated her fair and solicitous nature. She never forgot their birthdays, inquired about their families, and could be relied upon to keep their confidences. Banking customers equally admired her. She aided them in obtaining the best mortgage or loan rates and advised them on which accounts were best, given their personal circumstances. She could have taken advantage of them to increase the branch's numbers, but people were more important to her than profit. It humiliated her to even have it suggested she may have done something illegal.

As she considered her situation her cellphone began to ring. Smiling, she told the agent, "This is probably my husband."

He snorted. "I doubt it."

Laurel deflated when she realized he was correct, it wasn't Chaz. Caller ID showed it was her New York supervisor, Tom Underwood. She was uncertain if his call was routine, or he knew something was amiss. In either case she would have to tell him federal agents raided the bank. "Tom," she began, unable to hide her agitation. "There are FBI agents going through all our records."

"We know all about it. This is particularly important Laurel, say nothing to anyone."

She stepped away from the agents to avoid being overheard. "That shouldn't be too difficult, I don't know anything."

"We have our own people enroute and a lawyer for you. Corporate is in major damage control mode," he explained with concern in his voice.

She practically hissed her next question. "Can you at least tell me what they are searching for?"

"In a word," he replied, "embezzlement."

"At the bank? You know me better than that."

"The Feds don't know our history with you. We have total faith in your integrity," Tom said. "Chaz is another matter. I don't have all the details, but it appears he has broken more federal laws than I could enumerate."

Shocked, frightened, and feeling totally defeated, Laurel dropped her phone into her purse. She stared at the front door of the bank. It was still locked, but the key was in the deadbolt. She headed for it and starting to unlock it to leave.

The agent called out, "Where do you think you're going? We have more questions."

She stopped dead in her tracks, turned to face him and said with finality, "Call my lawyer."

People had begun to gather outside the bank. Her employees were understandably concerned, and customers wanted to conduct their financial business. They called out questions to her for which she had no answers.

"Was the bank robbed?" a young teller asked.

Laurel looked into her curious eyes and replied, "I certainly hope not."

The bank's head teller Janet Miller, one of Laurel's closest friends, reached out as Laurel passed her, touching her shoulder.

Laurel momentarily stopped to exchange glances but went ahead without speaking. She continued to walk the short distance to her home.

****

Her home on Maple Street had once been her haven. Situated on a large lot in one of the affluent sections of Bridgefield, it was close enough to the village to be within walking distance of everything while maintaining some degree of privacy. She and Chaz had been fortunate to have found it. Houses in the area seldom stayed on the market for more than a few days. Today it lost its sanctuary status.

Agents freely wandered the interior. When she walked through the door it sickened her to watch her things being touched and moved from their designated spots. She felt violated.

Agents carrying file boxes and computers, passed by her like she was invisible. Both she and Chaz often worked from home on their respective projects, but each had their own computer. The agents seized both. Though hers was one she used exclusively and would hold nothing incriminating, that did little for her current frame of mind.

She dropped heavily onto the sofa and stared absently into space, praying for indignant rage. She wanted to scream at the top of her lungs, throw a glass at the fireplace, and watch it smash into a million pieces. She would have enjoyed taking a sharp pair of scissors to Chaz's clothes.

She could not muster rage. Instead, all she felt was numbness. Her arms, legs, and even her brain felt numb. She managed to reach into her purse and retrieve her phone. She dialed Chaz's number again with no answer. She kept pushing the redial button, not that she thought he'd answer. She wanted to hear his voice, hoping he could give her a logical explanation. She was too astute to think he would have one.

As a financial advisor, her husband had held a position of trust with his clients and ready access to their money. The potential for fraud was clear. He had fewer checks and balances at his firm than she had at the bank. She had seen dozens of examples where unsuspecting clients, generally the elderly, had been cheated out of their lifesavings. It sickened her that her husband may be one of those perpetrators.

A female agent approached, speaking in a gentle voice. "We've completed our search, Mrs. Tanner. Here is an itemized list of everything we are removing from the house."

Saying nothing, Laurel reached for the paperwork. The agents left, leaving her with only disconcerting thoughts. The one comfort she had was the confidence she had done nothing wrong and would be completely exonerated. She knew Chaz to be a shrewd and even sometimes ruthless businessman, but she never thought he was a thief. Nevertheless, she refused to handle any of his banking needs for his company. She wanted a clear separation to avoid any impropriety. They had a joint checking and savings account with a modest balance at the Bridgefield Bank, and their mortgage, which was nearly paid off. The only other accounts she had at the bank were ones she'd shared with her mother. Her mother had died a few years earlier, but she uncharacteristically procrastinated on probating her will, feeling that as an only child, finalizing the estate was of no urgency.

As she tried to clear her head, the doorbell rang. She answered the door and was horrified to find reporters shoving cameras and microphones, in her face.

"Mrs. Tanner, can you tell us why Bridgefield Bank is closed?"

Another shouted, "We understand the FBI has raided the bank and your home."

"The citizens of Bridgefield have a right to know if their money has been misappropriated," a third said.

She did her best to sound composed. "If I had answers to your questions, I would gladly share them, but I don't. Please leave my property at once and do not return."

She closed and securely locked the door. After a moment, she discreetly peeked out one of the front windows and found them still milling along the sidewalk—but well off her property. She felt like a caged animal. She would have loved to escape to some place quiet and safe, but where could she go?

While she pondered escape, her phone rang. She was hesitant to answer but she was afraid it might be important. Tentatively she did answer with a noncommittal, "May I help you?"

"Mrs. Tanner, my name is Stuart Hoffman. I am an attorney from the New York office. I'm only a couple of miles from your home. May we meet?"

Laurel jumped at the chance for help. She confirmed her address with him and forewarned him about the reporters camped in front of her house. He was not deterred, when a few minutes later, he blared his car horn for them to move as he made his way up her driveway.

Mr. Hoffman was instantly surrounded by the news media and told them in a stern voice, "This is private property, and you are trespassing. We will be issuing a public statement, until that time, Mrs. Tanner is requesting privacy."

The throngs of reporters backed off as he went to the front door. Laurel practically pulled him through the threshold. She was not worried he was a reporter disguised as an attorney. He looked like every stereotypical lawyer she'd met from the New York office, impeccably dressed in an expensive dark suit and overcoat and comporting himself with confidence. He had a full head of silver-gray hair belying his age; she doubted he was yet fifty.

"Mrs. Tanner, I'm Stuart Hoffman," he said, extending his hand.

She prayed he understood the desperate situation she was in and would alleviate some of her anxiety. "I've never been so happy to see anyone. I don't know where to turn or what to do."

"That's why I'm here," Hoffman said. "To be clear, I'm here to represent you as it pertains to the bank and its entities."

"Aren't they one in the same?"

"Only partially. I'm afraid your legal problems will extend far beyond your position as bank president. Your husband has created a mess which I am only beginning to unravel. It will take a considerable amount of time and effort to figure things out."

"I'm sorry," she said. "Please, have a seat." Once they were settled on the leather tufted sofa, she asked, "Do you know where Chaz is?"

"I have no idea," he said. "It's conceivable the FBI may know, but it is highly unlikely they would share that information. How confident are you he has not perpetrated any kind of fraud at the bank?"

She shook her head. "If you had asked me that question yesterday, I would have said one hundred percent."

"And today?"

"I feel so blindsided; I now question everything

including my own name. Nevertheless, I'm ninety-nine percent certain. I love my husband, and he knows I would never compromise myself or the bank. It is probably the reason he disappeared without saying anything to me."

"The New York office is of the same opinion. They have unwavering faith in you. Unfortunately, that may be irrelevant. This whole situation has created a publicity nightmare."

Laurel knew he was right. All banking institutions were notoriously conservative. The slightest hint of scandal was to be avoided at all costs. "Are they going to fire me?" she asked, fearful of his answer.

"I'm not able to answer that question one way or another. I do know it would not be in anyone's best interest to do it now. It would imply your guilt, hence their negligence. I'm certain in either event you won't be returning to the Bridgefield Bank.

"Administrative leave?" she asked.

He nodded. "That's as good an explanation as any. They have sent their own auditors to work in conjunction with the FBI. The results will determine how everyone should proceed. If everything is in order, as you seem to think it is, then a final decision will be reached. In any event, the FBI will be done with what they need today, and the bank will be open tomorrow, just not with you."

Until now she withheld tears, but her resolve was giving way. "Do you know how utterly humiliating this is? I know I haven't done anything wrong, but somehow, I feel that I have. I won't be able to show my face in this town. These are the people I care about, those I've helped. Now they think I've betrayed them."

He reached out and took her hand. "I'd like to tell you this will all blow over, but small towns have long memories. That can work for or against you. If the people who matter believe in you, trust in that."

She laughed but it was without humor. "*Trust.* What's that? I once thought I knew the answers. I am such a fool."

Chapter Two

Stuart Hoffman left the house with the promise he would be in touch, hopefully with answers. Laurel felt utterly alone, a pariah with nowhere to turn. She needed to examine her life to figure out how she got to this point. She had been born the quintessential small town girl next door, and despite her rise to success, she remained true in her heart to those principles. She had her parents to thank for keeping her grounded while still encouraging her to be her best self.

Caroline and Jack Quincy could have been the model for parenting. They were people of modest means; however, they made up for it with love and steadfast devotion to their daughter. They recognized a superior intellect in Laurel and were determined their circumstances would never hinder her potential.

Jack worked at the nearby steel foundry. It was arduous work, but the salary supported their humble home and Laurel's educational needs. Periodic layoffs from the plant would be supplemented by Caroline taking odd jobs at the pharmacy or grocery store. They did not have everything they wanted but certainly everything they needed. When Laurel was accepted to Harvard, her parents were alternately thrilled and panicked. They wanted nothing to stand in her way. Her father postponed his retirement to help add to the scholarship she had received. It had been her greatest regret that he did not live long enough to see her graduate. The years of demanding work took its toll, and he died during her senior year of college. It had been her intention to contribute generously to their retirement to repay all they had done for her. That act of devotion would be to Caroline alone. She urged her daughter to continue at Harvard to receive her MBA, knowing it would increase her future opportunities.

Laurel let her mind focus on those simpler times. Her gaze gravitated to the framed photograph on her fireplace mantle. She and her mother were beaming with pride at Laurel's graduation. It had been bittersweet; bitter because her father was not there and sweet because he had helped make it happen. Her mother refused to let her feel depressed over her father's absence because it would have diminished the importance of her achievement.

"All we have ever wanted for you is to let you shine. It's your time," her mother told her after she received her MBA.

When an opportunity presented itself for Laurel to work abroad in international finance, her mother insisted she accept, telling her she would gain experience overseas which would lead to unending opportunities when she returned. It was that argument she used which convinced Laurel to go. When she came home, she would be in a better position to keep the promises she had made to herself to take care of her mother in style.

What her mother had not told her was her own health was failing. Caroline had managed to keep her heart condition a secret from Laurel for fear she would forego important business prospects. It was an unselfish decision she never regretted. Her daughter flourished, returning to many offers in New York City. It was there she met and fell in love with Chaz.

Laurel had been a serious student and an even more serious employee. She focused her entire attention toward her career leaving little time for romance. That changed when she met Charles Tanner at a charity function.

She had recently accepted an offer with Hudson International Finance Group, the fifth largest banking conglomerate in the country. Each year they sponsored an auction to raise money for the children's hospital. It was at one of these functions that she met Chaz Tanner. She later learned he was one of the most successful and controversial vice presidents of the investment company where he was employed. He took risks, but those risks usually yielded astounding results. His failures were admonished but largely overlooked. He was a man who knew what he wanted and let nothing get in his way.

The first time they met, he said, "If you're not busy later, would you like to get married?"

It was a pickup line that worked, and a few months later they eloped. Laurel had invited her mother to join them, but Caroline declined. Her decision had nothing to do with her opinion on their marriage because, as she often said, she sincerely liked Chaz. He had charmed his future mother-in-law like he did everyone else.

Laurel discovered months later her mother had secretly undergone heart bypass surgery. She kept that information from Laurel fearing she would take a leave of absence from her new job. She told Laurel she had her blessing, but she had developed an inner ear imbalance and flying was not advisable. She would have a wedding dinner for them when they returned.

Laurel and Chaz settled in their apartment in New York City and began married life perfectly content in their lives and careers. Laurel was rapidly rising in her career, and Chaz was seemingly as successful in his. The only downside for Laurel was the distance between her and her mother. Caroline could no longer keep her health issues a secret, which required Laurel to make frequent weekend trips home. It was only a short flight, but it was a strain on her and her mother. After consulting with Chaz, he was in complete agreement Caroline come to New York and live with them. He had only the highest regard for his mother-in-law and did not consider her an imposition. He had a less than cordial relationship with his family and appreciated the devotion his wife had for her mother. Caroline, on the other hand, could not be compelled to leave her home and friends.

"Mom, I'm worried sick every time I leave you. The cottage is too far from town and short on amenities."

Caroline smiled. "You make it sound like I live in the back country, hauling water from a stream. I'm comfortable here. You've seen to that. I've got my friends, and I drive back and forth to town. I'm too old to change my ways."

"Chaz and I have discussed it; we have plenty of room for you," Laurel said. "You'll love New York."

Her mother just laughed. "Did you actually rehearse that?"

Laurel laughed too. She knew her mother would have hated the city; she didn't like it much either, but it was where her opportunities lay. "It sounded better in my head. Seriously, though, I'm worried about you."

"Let's hold off on any decisions," Caroline suggested. "Things have a way of working out."

Laurel returned to New York plagued with worry. Her mother was everything to her, and she knew if something happened, she would blame herself. It was that exact feeling her mother had hoped to avoid by keeping her daughter ignorant about her health. Each was going to great lengths to be unselfish and neither had a solution.

Chaz often expressed concern for both his wife and mother-in-law. He deeply loved Laurel, and her mother by extension, and often reminded her of that. He stated several times he was amenable to anything that would make them happy but found it necessary to remind his wife of a few facts. "Your mother is a grown woman. Not only does she have the right to live her life in any manner she chooses, she has also earned it. I feel for both of you, I really do, but not everything can be micromanaged."

It was statements like that which made it difficult for Laurel to reconcile Chaz with his present-day actions. That was not the generous and caring person she had known. Certainly, she knew him to be shrewd and even hawkish in his business dealing. People seemed to either revere him for his financial acumen or dislike him. There was little middle ground. She could not accept he cleverly perpetrated a fraud. She was still looking for a reasonable explanation. There were, however, red flags she had missed.

The following day, after their conversation about her mother, they had to attend a mandatory cocktail party. Laurel and Chaz's respective firms sponsored a fundraiser for the head-trauma unit at one of Manhattan's leading hospitals. The last thing she was in a mood for was a cocktail party.

"How can I live the high life with my poor mother struggling with her health?" Laurel asked Chaz as she dressed for the event.

He reached out and embraced her. "We'll find a way, I promise."

Both he and her mother had been right about things working out. While mingling with the guests at the cocktail party, Chaz being Chaz ingratiated himself with fellow guests. He singled out people of importance and skillfully listened in on their conversations. It was something he had done for years and often yielded useful information even when he was not an active participant of the conversation. If he had been honest with himself, which he seldom was, it was the only way he learned valuable tidbits. He was successful, but many in the business did not trust him, with good reason. He was ruthless if he thought he could get ahead at someone else's expense. Laurel had a completely different reputation. Chaz had benefitted greatly from that reputation. People who were in their circle would actively avoid him but never wanted to hurt or slight Laurel. She had been oblivious to that fact, but Chaz, on some level, was not, and that evening was no exception.

When they returned to their apartment, he caught her completely off guard when he said, "I think I may have a mutually beneficial solution to your concerns about your mother."

"I can't imagine what that could be," she told him,

eager for his explanation.

"You know Ken Durant, right?"

"He was a vice president at your firm until he moved over to one of your competitors."

"That's correct. I overheard him say his father is selling his financial consulting business."

"What does that have to do with my mother?"

"It's in the nearby city, not more than thirty minutes from the township where your mother lives."

"Chaz, can you get to the point?"

He took a deep breath, then told her his plan. "I want to buy it and move."

She was dumbstruck. She didn't think there was a force on earth which could have induced him to leave Manhattan and his lucrative position.

"Hear me out..." He started with such animation he nearly knocked over a lamp. "I'm tired of making money for other people. If I bought Durant's firm, I'd be my own boss with limitless possibilities."

She wasn't against the idea, but there were too many unknowns for her to give him an informed opinion. "What do you know about Durant's bottom line? You'd have to do a complete audit before you could even offer him a price. Let's be realistic, even if it is a good deal, you still wouldn't make the kind of money you do here."

"We wouldn't need as much money if we weren't in Manhattan, and how much do we really need anyway? I know you've never been a city girl. We could find a nice house in the suburbs close to your mother, commute back and forth."

"We? What could I do?"

"There are banks there, too, you know."

She laughed. "Not like what I'm doing here. I'd have a huge pay cut, too."

"Does that really matter to you?" he reasoned. "We could be big fish in a small pond. We're just another insignificant up and coming couple in Manhattan."

Laurel wasn't against the idea—in fact it appealed to her; however, her husband was often impetuous. She both loved and distrusted that quality in him. He would become excited over one of his plans only to fall on his face, sometimes losing money for his firm. She was always cautious and steady and liked it when he would pull her from her comfort zone. She would follow him, but not blindly.

Smiling, she replied, "I think it's worth exploring. We'll be starting a family soon, and the city is not the place I want to raise our children. I loved my childhood, and I don't want to become one of those career-obsessed parents."

He ran to her and gave her a hug. "That's my girl."

"Wait," she said, pulling back from his grip. "I want hard numbers and a solid plan."

Not wanting to get Caroline's hopes up, Laurel mentioned nothing to her mother. She wanted to make sure Chaz's enthusiasm didn't wane or his plan not be feasible. She also had to take into consideration her own career. She decided her best course of action was no course of action. She was comfortably employed, and if Chaz changed his mind, it would have a negligible effect on her.

Laurel watched her husband throw himself into exploring Durant Financial. They were not a large firm but solid and profitable, he'd told her. And though he met with them several times, he said he felt as though they weren't enthusiastic about the sale.

Durant was a practical man, and Chaz was able to guarantee his purchase of the company with securities which satisfied his demands. Once he had done that, Laurel was faced with her own career options. She made an appointment with her superiors to discuss her future and was warmly greeted when they asked, "Why have you called this conference?"

She was little nervous but replied, "I'm tendering my resignation."

Her immediate supervisor looked stunned. "Laurel, you are one of our rising stars. Is something wrong? Why are you leaving?"

"Family matters. You know my mother has been ill, and she needs me to be closer. Bringing her to Manhattan wasn't an option and I owe her," she explained. "She and my father sacrificed everything for my education. It's time I repay her."

"What about Chaz?" her boss asked. "I can't see him leaving New York City."

"It was his idea. He wanted a business of his own, and he purchased Durant Financial."

The three executives exchanged silent looks. Because this concerned her, she asked, "Do you know something I don't?"

Quickly her boss replied, "No, at least nothing negative about Durant."

Shaking her head, she asked, "Then what?"

One of the other executives said diplomatically, "Do you think Chaz is up to this new venture?"

"Why wouldn't he be? He put this whole deal together nearly single-handedly."

"We are aware he has had some failures, and we

would hate to see you have to pay for them. This will be an enormous change for each of you. Have you thought about what's next for you?"

She knew they were right to be concerned. Someone as dedicated and thoughtful as Laurel would be lost without career options. "I'm open to suggestions," she said.

"Let us do some talking among ourselves and get back to you," her boss told her.

Chapter Three

After a long discussion, the executive board members called Laurel back into the room. In their own way they informed her, they were prepared to present her with a career option, keeping her under their umbrella of banking interests.

"Are you familiar with Bridgefield?" one of the members asked.

"Of course, it's not more than fifteen minutes from my childhood home."

"We'd like to offer you the presidency of our branch there. It has a lot of potential, for a small-town bank. We recently acquired it, and it may eventually be combined with some other independent banks. It will give you the opportunity to be on the ground floor of something larger. It's not Manhattan, but it may serve you well."

She was elated. "It sounds perfect. Chaz and I could buy a house in Bridgefield; he could commute to the city. My mother would be nearby as well."

"Buying a house in Bridgefield would be advisable," they told her. "We like our executives to live in the community. It builds trust and transparency."

It was the first time she was totally comfortable with the move. Things were falling into place. It would take several months before they could completely wrap up their lives in Manhattan. Chaz was met with no resistance from his employer. Much to his chagrin, they started at once to look for his replacement. He told her he had made some enemies at work, which was even more reason for him to become his own boss.

Chaz was in his element as boss. Several members of the firm remained, while others retired after Durant sold the company. Chaz's need for recognition made him want to replace the name of Durant with his own, but his business sense prevailed. Durant was well respected, and the name meant something. It was for that reason Durant went ahead with trepidation because it was a condition of the sale.

Chaz may have been a ruthless businessman, but he could also be charming and personable. His employees appreciated his sense of humor and interest in their personal lives. He made it a point to glean details of their lives. He needed their goodwill to be successful, and they needed a paycheck so they would stroke his ego whenever the occasion should arise. The arrangement made his new business run smoothly and everyone seemed content.

Laurel was on a similar path. She did not have the luxury of not being accountable to someone as was her husband. She had to adhere to corporate oversight; however, as the branch president she could set the tone. She was aware of the fact she was stepping into the position which had been previously held by the same man for twenty years. He was beloved by the employees and community at large. Any attempt, on her part, to radically change the way the bank was run would be poorly received. Her youth and gender should not have been an issue, but it generally became one.

She had navigated that before and knew efficiency

and sincerity would quickly overcome any preconceived prejudices that may exist. She had been in the banking world long enough to know corporate outsiders were looked upon with suspicion. It made the employees uneasy. They were concerned that the corporate bottom line would be more important than the concerns of their employees. She did everything in her power to assure them she would not let that happen. It would later prove beneficial when she had to rebuild her life. The goodwill of the community was important.

Before Laurel assumed her position, she literally dissected the banks records. It was the only bank in town, and although profitable, it lacked an organizational plan, which was the cornerstone of her business style. The bank had woefully neglected to update their computer system both for the convenience of the bank and customers. It was a common occurrence at smaller, independent institutions. They did not have the resources available to them that the parent banking system enjoyed. It had been her priority to arrange for the upgrade.

At first the bank employees were upset by the changes, but once she arranged for instruction, they admitted to her they found the new system was far more efficient and made their jobs easier. It reduced errors, automatically backed-up data, and protected the bank from intentional manipulation. Little did Laurel know at the time this one small effort in efficiency would protect her from her husband's betrayal.

Pleased with their new careers, Laurel and Chaz worked longer hours, but that was due to the adjustment curve they each experienced. They had never been happier, and each anticipated a bright future.

The couple had been in Bridgefield for nearly two years when Caroline Quincy died. Laurel made her usual morning call to her mother, but she did not answer. That was not necessarily a concern because sometimes her mother was outside or in the shower so she would call back. It became a concern when repeated calls were not answered; Laurel then drove to the cottage. The door was locked, so she let herself in. She was relieved when she heard the television on in the bedroom, but that relief was short lived. Her mother had peacefully died in bed while watching television. Laurel was bereft. She had only been slightly consoled that it had been swift and with the knowledge they had the last couple of years together.

Friends and co-workers gathered around her. They had been acquainted with Laurel's mother and knew that had played a large part in her return to the area. She had been urged to take some time off, but she refused. After the funeral, she went to her mother's house, cleaned out the refrigerator, packed up a few personal items, and locked the doors. She couldn't bear to return to a place which was the essence of her mother and her childhood.

Chaz was loving, understanding, and wanted to help in any way he could, but only time would hopefully be her friend. She threw herself almost entirely into the bank as did Chaz with his financial company. Laurel was pleased at the expansion of the bank. Under her leadership, it had increased its value by a third. They had expanded to two nearby townships, and although slow in the beginning, they had gained accounts justifying the expansion. Laurel's New York superiors extended her position to be the direct supervisor of the new acquisitions. If her mother had been living, she probably would not have accepted the added responsibility, but she needed the distraction. As considerate as Chaz had been after her mother's death, he found himself growing his business. He was working longer hours, and it required him to often travel.

He was proud of his success and wanted to reap the rewards. He bought custom-made suits, an expensive car, and urged Laurel to move to a new home more in keeping with his financial status. She was pleased he was doing so well, but she loved her home and had no desire to move.

He protested. "This place served its purpose, but we can afford something larger."

"Why? It's only the two of us, at least for now. The house is nearly paid for, so why would you want to go into further debt? You're the financial guy, surely you see the logic in staying here."

"If you sold your mother's place, we could put that money into a home large enough for a family," he reasoned. "It's a modest cottage, but you put a lot of money into it when your mother was living there. It's close enough to the city to be considered a weekend getaway. People would pay good money for it."

It had now been three years since her mother's death, and she still was not able to consider selling it. She hadn't even officially put the house in her name. She paid the taxes and kept the utilities on but never returned except to periodically check on it.

Her answer was not open for discussion. "No."

Chaz never directly confronted her on the sale of the cottage but occasionally made general references that he could invest the money for her future benefit.

She ignored his comments. It was one of the few areas of their relationship in which she remained resolute.

****

The days that followed the FBI raid seemed like years. Laurel spoke to no one except her attorney and the banking supervisors in New York. It was quickly determined she had committed no crimes related to her role as bank president. Her diligence and efficiency made it possible for auditors to determine that conclusion with little difficulty. It was enough to have been exonerated by the bank to keep the reporters away from her door. She was not totally in the clear, however. Her involvement with Chaz's company had yet to be decided. As her husband, he had her listed on many documents, though she had no active participation in his firm.

She felt isolated while waiting for news about her husband and what she would do next. She had many friends who tried to contact her, but her embarrassment was so great she avoided all of them. Once the corporate offices were satisfied with her innocence, they agreed to pay Stuart Hoffman to continue helping her in her legal woes. It was guilt money because they were replacing her. They were honest and direct and told her she was a liability even though she was cleared of any mismanagement. The fact there was still a pending investigation that tied her to Chaz was reason enough to let her go.

It was Stuart who delivered the unwelcome news. He sat across from her at her dining room table, shuffling ponderous amounts of legal papers. "I'm very sorry, Laurel."

She felt so defeated she barely found the breath to

speak. "It's not your fault, and I cannot blame my superiors," she murmured, resigned to the inevitable. "This has been Chaz's and my mistake."

He reached over to squeeze her hand. "I don't know how or why you would blame yourself. You had no part in any of this. The more I pore through the records and things provided by the FBI, the more I know you were ignorant of anything he did."

She stood and walked to the window, staring out absently for a few moments before returning to her seat. "That's just it. I'm too savvy to have not recognized the signs. He was living beyond his means and justifying it. I should have known better."

"That's water under the bridge," he began. "Now we have to think only of you and straighten out your financial mess."

Feeling terribly sad, she asked, "What are the damages?"

He leaned back in his chair, removed his eyeglasses to rub his eyes and sighed. "I'm afraid considerable, but let's start with what you do have. The bank will cover all my expenses and continue your benefits until the end of the year."

She was still feeling a little detached from their conversation. A part of her wanted to believe it was all a bad dream, but she was doing her best to be pragmatic. "That's more than fair under the circumstances."

He picked up a manilla folder and opened it. "You have the vested rights in your pension. You are a young woman and that doesn't help you much now."

"By the time I'm of retirement age, it will mean something and eventually I'll get another job. At least I can cash in some of Chaz's and my negotiables."

The blank expression on Stuart's face worried her. "Can't I?"

He took a deep breath. "There's nothing left. Chaz cashed everything in. Your money is gone along with all his client's money."

"Everything?" she choked. "All the CDs and money market accounts?"

"What he couldn't get his hands on, the Feds have seized. There will be an endless parade of lawsuits."

"What about this house? Not that I can ever live in this town any longer."

He delivered more bad news. "Even if it wasn't part of the seizure, there's no equity in."

She was certain he must have been mistaken. "Of course, there is. We only had a small mortgage left."

"Chaz took out a second mortgage. Even if you wanted to keep it, there's nothing worth fighting for."

"No, that's not possible. The house is in both our names. He couldn't get a mortgage without my signature."

He just stared at her with a sad look on his face. Finally, she realized what Chaz had done and horror filled her. "He forged my signature."

It was Stuart's turn to stand and walk. She watched anxiously as he paced the room before he spoke. "I'm afraid he forged a lot of signatures. No one, including you, is likely to see a dime."

Suddenly nauseous, she ran for the kitchen sink. After vomiting everything she'd eaten and drank over the past hours, she grabbed a glass from the cabinet and downed a cold water to clear the taste in her mouth. When she returned, she was composed. "I can start over somehow, but what about the people he cheated? Most of his clients were elderly."

His smile was filled with sorrow. "I applaud your compassion, but they are on their own just as you are. I doubt they would see it that way, but you're every bit as much a victim as they."

Salty tears began to drip down her face. "Where do I begin?"

"It's not a total loss," he assured her. "As I went through the paperwork, I discovered a deed. It has the name of Caroline Quincy on it. There were also a couple of small bank accounts with that name and yours on it. Is Caroline your mother?"

She nodded. "I'm an only child. She left it to me; I just never did anything with it except pay the taxes on the cottage and make sure it was in repair."

"Your procrastination could very well be your saving grace. I don't know why you did not probate her estate, but it will work to your advantage. There is no other heir and no one to contest it. Until this mess is resolved, let's leave it that way. You will at least have a roof over your head."

A smile crossed Laurel's lips as she thought of her mother. "Somehow my mother always saved the day. God bless her."

"My first order of business is to get you a divorce. You want to distance yourself from Chaz as completely and quickly as possible. I recommend you return to your maiden name."

"How can we do that when we don't even know where he is?"

He waved his hand in a dismissive manner. "That's the least of your worries. A judge will grant you a divorce on several grounds. I'll take care of that."

Seeing the wisdom in his advice, she wanted to sever all ties to Chaz. "How long will all of this take?"

"A few weeks for the divorce with a sympathetic judge. I'll have letters of agreement concerning your house and other jointly owned assets drawn up. Of course, most of that has been seized, but I'm hoping to salvage your credit by voluntarily not contesting ownership. The fight to hang onto anything is not worth it. Any legal matters involving Chaz could potentially drag on for years."

"Years?" She heard herself shout as it echoed through her ears.

"Yes, but I'm confident that the FBI will clear you of any culpability in the next few months. When that happens, the corporate offices may find some other position for you, maybe even overseas. They still believe in you, you know."

"Am I going to be thrown out of here soon?" she asked, looking around the house she's shared with her soon to be ex-husband.

"The people I'm dealing with aren't heartless. They will, however, want to take possession as soon as you sign the voluntary foreclosure. Figure out what you want to do and when you want to do it."

She snorted a response. "No pressure there."

"Look," he began, "I need to say this; you're a woman of honor and did not deserve any of this. It may seem insurmountable now, but the worst is behind you. It was your integrity that ultimately saved you, and it's that same integrity that will propel you forward."

Even in her despair she recognized the importance of all the effort Stuart was making on her behalf. "I'd have been lost without your help."

"There is still more to do. Even after this is all over, you can feel free to ask me to help in other matters. I'll even do it pro bono."

"I'll remember that when I'm standing in the food line," she said sarcastically.

He smiled and replied lightly. "I hardly think a Harvard MBA will starve to death. You'll land on your feet, especially if you go back to work for corporate."

"I'm not sure I will. There is a part of me which thinks I got ahead of myself. I needed to be humbled."

Stuart stuffed the files back into his briefcase and headed for the door, but as he was leaving, he turned to her. "You've always been humble, Laurel. Right now, you're just a little lost."

Chapter Four

Laurel saw no point in delaying the move until after she lost possession of the house. She drove her car, one of her few possessions which was not seized or otherwise entangled, and went to her mother's cottage in Rose Hill.

Once there, she stood on the porch and took a deep breath before entering. Knowing this was now her permanent home, she did not know how she would feel going inside. She was pleasantly surprised. Although the cottage needed airing out and a good cleaning, she had the sensation of being hugged. She even imagined she could smell her mother's bread baking. After weeks of uncertainty and emotional turmoil, she was home.

She walked through the rooms, touching objects tenderly as she passed them and stopped at her mother's bedroom. Even the room where she had died was not oppressive. Her parents had lived with love in their home, and they died with that same love. She would give what little she had left to see them again but would not wish the anguish they would have felt over her humiliation.

There was a photograph of her parents on their wedding day sitting on the fireplace mantel. She picked it up and gazed upon it, saying to them, "I need you so much. If there is any way to share your wisdom, please send it my way."

She spent the next week cleaning and organizing both the cottage and her house in Bridgefield. She took little from that house. There were too many negative memories, which she refused to bring to the cottage. She might have sold many of the pieces of furniture and china but chose to donate it to charity. She could have used the money any sales would have brought, but it felt tainted. If she were going to start over, it needed to be on her own terms. When she locked the front door for the last time, she mailed the key to Stuart and never looked back.

As desirable as it had been to leave Manhattan to be closer to her mother, she now wished the cottage in Rose Hill was a greater distance from Bridgefield. She was a couple of towns away but still close enough to run into people she knew and who knew, at least in part, what had happened. Her mother's neighbors were kind and blessedly silent about Laurel's occupancy of the cottage.

The elderly woman next door stopped by with an apple pie. "It's good to see someone in your mother's house. We've all missed her, and I'm sure you will bring the place back to life."

Laurel thanked her, but in her mind, she was thinking, *Just as soon as I bring myself back.*

There was little she wanted to change at the cottage. After Laurel moved to Bridgefield, she took her mother shopping and they had redecorated much of the cottage and made necessary updates. The room which had been altered the least was her childhood bedroom. It had been nearly double the size of her parents' bedroom. Her father had knocked down the wall between her room and the third bedroom making it one large space. Laurel had been such a serious student, with volumes of books, her parents wanted her to have a sanctuary to study. She took it for granted at the time but now felt guilty about it.

She'd even asked her mother, "Why didn't you and Dad move into my room when I left? It's such a beautiful space."

Her mother had replied, "It seemed almost sacrilegious."

Laurel understood her point, she felt much the same way about her parents' bedroom. She was pleased, however, that her mother had made use of the computer she had left behind. It surprised her how proficient she had become. In the years after her husband had died, Caroline occupied some of her time by playing around on it until she became self-taught. She stayed connected with friends and family members, exchanging photos and stories. When Laurel saw how outdated it was, she bought her a new state of the art desktop model. Now, with a few downloads, it would serve Laurel well. She entertained no hope her own would be returned to her by the Feds, and she needed a computer to function.

Her parents had kept all her academic awards and achievements, either hanging them on walls or putting them into frames on the desk and bookcases. Those were the first things she removed, not wanting to be reminded of where she had come from only to have disgraced herself. She placed them in a plastic tote to haul up to the attic. She momentarily held her framed Harvard diploma. She was going to drop it into the box with the others but stopped when she read her name: *Laurel Abigail Quincy*.

It was not Laurel Tanner and she realized she had to remember that. She was not that woman any longer, she was the one on her diploma. She did not place it in the box, nor did she hang it back on the wall. She took it into her parents' bedroom and placed it on a dresser. It was their achievement as much as hers and she wanted to honor that.

She spent much of the day unpacking the boxes she had brought with her. It seemed almost pathetic that her life had been condensed into a half dozen of them. Ironically, they consisted largely of gifts from her parents. They were now home just as she was. It gave her an odd sense of peace, something she had been lacking for months.

She opened the stairway door to the attic and proceeded to drag boxes up to the dusty and uninsulated attic. It was far from an empty space. It was filled with postponed decisions. She suspected if her parents hadn't been in ill health, they probably would have cleaned it out long ago. She certainly had the time to do it and hoped it would even be cathartic. She was pleased that the boxes had at least been marked. It would accelerate her cleaning process. The box which stopped her in her tracks was marked *photo albums*. She slid it over to the stairs and carried it down to examine its contents. She hesitated for a few minutes to decide if she was ready for a trip down memory lane. She concluded it would be part of her healing process.

Boxes were not simply filled with her memories; they were those of people she barely remembered or never knew. Grandparents, great-grandparents, aunts, uncles, and cousins. She stared into their faces and smiled as she wondered what their hopes and dreams had been. She appreciated the time someone had spent labeling the pictures with names and dates. Growing up she had always focused on the future. She was ambitious and eager to succeed, so giving thought to the people who came before her never entered her mind. It suddenly took on a measure of importance. It didn't matter if they were descendants of kings, paupers, or thieves; they had a life and a story. She wondered what they would tell her if they could. She found photographs of her parents as babies sitting on their grandparents' lap. Many of her relatives were dressed in uniform. They dated from Vietnam to a Civil War photo of a many-great uncle.

She felt almost foolish in her self-pity. If they could survive, she could. It occurred to her that most of her relatives had lived in the immediate vicinity. She could not recall her parents ever speaking of that, or if they had, would she have paid attention? She suddenly realized she knew little of her own parents. They were simply Mom and Dad, and she never thought beyond that relationship. She adored them, helped in any way she could financially, but she had never asked them about their hopes and dreams, fears, and victories. The tears she had not shed for herself she now shed for them. She had hoped they were not disappointed she never asked, and now it was too late. She had comforted many friends who had lost a parent or grandparent and nearly every one of them had said, "I wish I would have asked them about…"

As she looked at her parents' wedding photo, she tried to fill in the blanks. She stared at her mother's dress. Why did it look familiar to her? She dug through the box and found it was the same dress her grandmother had worn, then a sense of horror struck her. She ran into her mother's bedroom and found the album that had not been placed in the dusty attic. She grabbed the one she knew had pictures of her throughout her high school years. She found her senior prom photo. The dress she was wearing was her mother's and grandmother's wedding dress. It had been substantially altered to modernize it, but the embroidery was unquestionably the same dress.

She recalled that time extremely well. She had been accepted into Harvard, and although she received a scholastic scholarship, it did not cover everything. Her parents would never discuss what their contribution had been, but the timing couldn't have been worse. The steel plant where her father had been employed was involved in a union strike and money had been tight. Laurel could remember wanting a new dress for the prom. Her high school boyfriend had come from an academic family with superior resources to her family. She cringed at how superficial she had been at wanting a new gown. She couldn't fully understand it was not within her parents' means. Her mother promised her she would find a suitable compromise.

She now realized it had been the wedding dress. Laurel knew it was not something from a department store, but it was beautiful in its intricate embroidery. Caroline probably thought she would one day wear it on her own wedding day. Instead, she and Chaz exchanged vows on a sunny beach.

"Oh, Mom," she said aloud. "If I had only known."

That night, Laurel wrestled with her conscience over these newfound realizations. She had no children of her own, so she could only imagine the sacrifice her mother made. If she had been in a frame of mind where she wasn't so hard on herself, she would have understood her mother's love for her was more important than a dress. Her mother had proven that countless times.

Feeling the need to apologize, she could have stood in the center of her mother's bedroom and said it aloud, but she wanted to go to the place she knew she could find her, or at least her earthly remains. She had not visited the cemetery since the day of her mother's funeral, yet another guilt trip.

Pioneer Cemetery was just that; a place founded by the early settlers to bury their families. It was acres upon acres of rolling hills lovingly dedicated to all who had come before her. The cemetery had become a history lesson to tourists and residents. Despite the thousands of graves, it was considered more of a park than a cemetery. There were endless varieties of trees and shrubs which attracted ample birdwatchers. The Audubon Society had even featured a story on the cemetery. The duck pond held a mixed variety of not just ducks but swans. Children delighted in tossing them food. Joggers and people walking their dogs were a constant sight on the many lanes and driveways.

Many years ago, a foresighted developer built a road on the north end of the cemetery where eager homeowners built their houses. It was near that location Laurel's parents were buried. It was the oldest section, and she was only now realizing that was because many of her ancestors were buried there as well. The plots had undoubtedly been in the family for generations.

She was embarrassed that it took her nearly a half hour to find her parents' grave. When she found it, she knelt and placed a bouquet of wildflowers on it. She traced their names in the headstone and sighed. "I'm so sorry if I disappointed you."

She stood up and took the time to take in the serenity and beauty of what was around her. She felt its spirituality, and she vowed she would return. It was not just a place of death but filled with artistic beauty from the intricate headstones to the natural wonders. It was obvious all the people who took advantage of that every day realized that fact.

She turned to walk back toward her car when she stumbled over a tree root. She fell, striking her head on the edge of her parents' headstone. When she lifted her head, the first thing she saw was a pair of pink fuzzy slippers. She continued to lift her head and a pink full-length bathrobe which appeared to be worn by an elderly woman who rested on the edge of a headstone.

"I saw you fall, dear," the old one said. "Are you all right?"

"I'm not sure. Where did you come from?" Laurel asked. The woman was hardly dressed for a walk in a public place.

There was a carefree disarming essence to the old woman. If it had not been for her snow-white hair and a gracefully lined face, Laurel would have taken her for someone much younger—even her voice carried a youthful note.

"Oh..." the old one said with a blithe wave of one hand, "I reside nearby."

Nodding in pain, she remembered the houses in the development, then rubbed her aching head and found blood on her hand. "How bad is this?" she asked the woman.

After carefully examining Laurel's head, she whooped with laughter. "You'll live, unlike most of the people here."

Laurel nodded. "Do you often walk around the cemetery dressed in your bathrobe?"

"Sweetie, when you're on the wrong side of middle-age like me, you might as well be invisible. If I ran through here buck-naked, no one would notice."

Getting into a sitting position against her parents' headstone, Laurel replied, "Oh, I doubt that."

The old woman asked, "Is there something I can do for you?"

"No, as usual I feel foolish. I'll gather myself together in a couple of minutes. My car is just over there," she said, pointing to the nearby cement path.

With a smirk, the woman said, "You know there is a cute young doctor who jogs through here every day. I know for a fact he's single. Maybe you could flag him down."

"Pick up a man in a cemetery? For all you know, I might be married with six kids."

Cocking her head to one side the woman replied, "Then a cemetery is the last place you'd be first thing in the morning."

Despite the circumstances, Laurel found herself enjoying this odd woman. "You are."

"I'm old and have no life."

"In any event, thank you for your concern, but I'll be fine."

"Okay, I'll leave you to your headache."

Laurel watched the woman walk toward the development before placing her head in her hands to try to hold off on the urge to vomit. When she felt steady, she stood to walk in the direction of her car. Just as she reached the path a jogger passed by.

Stopping, then turning, he gestured at her face. "What happened to you?"

"Do you want the long story or the short one?"

"I guess the short one."

"Stupidity."

He grinned. "That's generally the reason."

"Don't tell me you're a doctor."

His eyes widened. "How did you know?"

She didn't, it was shot in the dark after what the old woman told her.

"Educated guess."

"Do you mind if I take a look?" he asked with continued concern.

She was too nauseous to object. "Go for it."

He stepped closer. "The wound is still oozing. I have my medical bag in my car, but it's parked at the entrance. Wait here and I'll drive back."

"That's all right. I'll go home and clean it up," she answered.

He had a stern tone to his voice when he said, "Just wait here. I'll be back in a couple of minutes."

She already felt like a complete idiot and simply wanted to go home, but he was being so considerate she didn't want to duck out on him. In less than five minutes, he was back with his car and medical bag. He took her to his car and had her sit in the back seat as he cleansed her head with an antiseptic wipe.

"Holy crap that hurts!" She jolted her head backward. "Did you dip that thing in kerosene?"

He grinned. "You obviously don't know the difference between kerosene and gasoline."

"And what third world country did you get your medical degree from?" she asked, not to be insulting but to distract from her discomfort.

Seeming to be unoffended he shrugged. "I didn't exactly graduate, but I came close. Margaritaville Medical University is highly regarded."

She smiled at his successful attempt at humor. "That's comforting."

"I'll put some surgical tape on it, but it's borderline if you need a couple of sutures. There is a clinic in town."

"I think I'll just go home and take some aspirin."

"How far do you have to drive?" he asked. "You shouldn't be driving after a head injury."

"Five miles. I live on Winston Creek Road."

"Really? I'm on the next road over. I'd feel better if I followed you home. If you die after that point, it's on you."

She laughed. "You must have actually graduated from Margaritaville."

"I didn't graduate, remember?"

He did follow her to her driveway but waved as she pulled in. She was sincerely grateful he had not followed her into the driveway because she didn't feel well and equally grateful he did not try to impose himself on her. She was a long way from wanting to deal with another human being, especially a man.

She felt a strong urge to climb back into bed, but it was not even nine o'clock in the morning. That urge redoubled itself when she received a call from Stuart who announced, "You are now officially divorced."

She needed that last piece of closure of a divorce from Chaz, not only legally, but spiritually. It was disconcerting to her she had to face one more failure. She did not immediately respond but when she did, she asked him, "Do you know anything about where he is?"

"Does it matter?"

She hesitated before speaking. "I think it does."

"All right, I'll tell you what my sources told me. He knew his arrest was imminent. He had stalled so long everything was catching up. He fled to a country which will not extradite him to the States."

"Great," she began, totally disgusted, "he sits in luxury on some beach spending my money and that of dozens of others."

"If it's any consolation," Stuart said, "I don't think he has much of it left."

"How could that be?"

"I've learned Chaz didn't start out being a thief. It would appear he made a series of bad investments and was basically using a pyramid scheme to recover."

"That rarely works. I've seen it in other bank fraud cases."

"Exactly; his last-ditch effort was the money he was able to get from your assets. That's probably what he's living on."

"It was a fair amount of money but not enough to sustain him for the rest of his life. Even if he's in a country where it would go further, he'd have to eventually get a job."

"From what I could glean from reading between the lines," Stuart said, "I think he really believed he could have recovered."

She agreed with his assessment, though it was reluctant. "That sounds more like him. He used to be a kind and thoughtful man, a little full of himself, but loving. If he had been honest with me, there may have been something we could have done."

"Laurel, he was too far astray. Honesty might have saved him some jail time, but he would still have to be held accountable."

"I know. I had hoped better from him."

"Chaz is no longer your problem. He'll have to make or not make amends on his own. I'll send you the final papers while you put him in your past."

"Easier said than done. Thank you, Stuart. I'm sure we'll be in touch." She hung up the phone feeling a sense of ambivalence.

Her head was beginning to throb like a bass drum. She went to the bathroom mirror to take a closer look. The doctor may have been right about her needing a suture, but she cleansed the wound, put some antiseptic cream on it, and covered it with a bandage. It looked as if she may even have the beginnings of a black eye. She then popped a couple of aspirin and stretched out on her bed. She must have fallen asleep because she was startled awake by the doorbell. It was her mail carrier with a registered letter she had to put her signature on before accepting it.

She was afraid to even look; a registered letter seldom meant anything good. It wasn't as bad as she had feared. The corporate office had sent her a much-needed severance check. They had been generous, and it should sustain her until she found future employment. At least she had a comfortable roof over her head and no immediate matters she had to attend to.

She went outside to get some fresh air and realized the yard was a mess. She never renewed the lawn contract after the winter, and considering her new circumstances, she certainly wasn't going to spend unnecessary money. She wasn't a stranger to lawn work. When she was living at home, she mowed the lawn and pulled weeds in the flowerbeds. It was never a necessity living in Manhattan, and even her home in Bridgefield had a lawn service. There was a small tractor mower in the garage, but she knew it hadn't been used in years. Her mother enjoyed mowing the lawn, however she hired the neighbors' grandson to perform the more taxing work.

Laurel walked over to the mower and wondered if it even had any gas in it and if it did how old was it? She was afraid to even try to start it within the confines of the garage, so she slipped the gear into neutral and rolled it outside. It was an inexpensive mower and didn't even have a gas gauge. She opened the gas cap and saw a minimal amount of gas in the tank. Taking the *nothing ventured, nothing gained* approach, she tried to start it.

The engine wanted to start, but it was clear to her the battery was on its way out. She decided to go into town and buy fresh gasoline and a new battery. Many of her childhood skills had been dormant but filling a gas tank and replacing a lawn mower battery were within her skill set.

As she filled the gas can she heard a voice. It was the doctor from the cemetery. "You must be feeling better."

"Hi," she said, genuinely surprised to see him. "I want to apologize. I'm not normally so rude, and you were only trying to help me."

He seemed puzzled. "You weren't rude. In fact, I thought you were quite amusing."

She was relieved she had not offended him. She wasn't even sure what she had said to him. "Oh good. My head hurt so bad I hardly remember anything."

In a tone she would have expected from a doctor he said, "Are you sure you feel all right? You could have had a concussion."

She laughed aloud, something that had been missing in her life recently. "I would hardly know the difference, these days."

His tone was lighter. "That bad?"

"That bad."

"I've had a few of those times myself. By the way, my name is David Bradford."

"I'm Laurel." She hesitated, nearly using the name Tanner. "Quincy."

"You must have hit your head pretty hard; you sound like you aren't sure," he joked.

She kept her laugh light. "I'm not. It's a story for another day."

"What are you doing with the gas can?"

She looked down at the now-filled can. "I think I'm going to mow my lawn if the lawnmower works."

In an amused tone he asked, "You aren't sure about that either?"

"Nope. It was my mother's, and I don't know the last time it was used. It would be my luck that it would blow up on me."

"Do you want me to look at it?"

"Are you a lawnmower surgeon?"

"Pediatrician. The lawnmower should be easier to deal with."

She smiled. "I appreciate the offer, but I try not to impose on someone more than once a day."

"I offered; you didn't ask."

"Honestly, I don't even know if the old thing will work. I'm taking my best crack at it with a new battery and gas."

"What were you doing before to cut the grass?"

"My mother did it until she died. After that, I hired a yard service before I moved into her house."

He nodded. "Now that you live there, you feel like you should be doing it yourself like your mother did?"

Shaking her head. "Something like that. I've gotten too far away from manual labor, so I think it's time to get my hands dirty again."

"After med school and I started my practice, I was working too many hours. I was dispensing advice to parents that I wasn't taking myself. I would tell them, 'Get your kids away from the video games and out in the fresh air.' "

"You don't strike me as video game addict."

In an amazingly casual tone, he remarked, "Work was my video game addiction. Everyone has their poison. It wasn't until I had what the experts suspect was a heart attack that I made changes."

"Heart attack? You seem kind of young for that."

"It can happen any time to anyone, but it was just stress. That's why I started jogging. It's good exercise, I'm in the fresh air, and it really clears my head. It's incredible how clearly you can think if you aren't distracted by other things."

"I was thinking the same thing about mowing, although I'll have to listen to the engine drone in my ears."

He picked up her gasoline can and gallantly placed it in her trunk before saying, "If you have any problems with it, I'd be happy to take a look at it."

He pulled out his wallet and retrieved a business card. "My number is on here."

She thanked him but had no intentions of bothering him with the vagaries of starting a lawnmower.

Chapter Five

Laurel decided to tackle the lawnmower first thing in the morning when her head would not hurt as much, and she had more energy. It only took a few minutes to disconnect the old battery, replace it with the new one, and fill the tank with fresh gas.

She hopped on the mower and said aloud, "Here goes nothing," then turned the key. Much to her shock and relief, it promptly started. It may have seemed silly, but the satisfaction it gave her that she got it running boosted her spirit. It was symbolic of where she wanted to direct her life. She had a problem, she solved it on her own and could reap its reward. The fact that the reward was cutting grass did not matter, it was her victory.

As she traversed the lawn, spewing grass clippings everywhere, she let her mind wander, trying to examine how she got to this point. How did Chaz deceive her without her knowledge? She realized the bank had every right to dismiss her based simply on her ignorance. They had completely exonerated her, and she was well on her way of having the same result by the FBI, but that was not enough. She had a character flaw which allowed it to happen. Reaching into her past to search for it she concluded her parents were partially responsible. Not because they had done anything wrong, but they did too many things right. She had many friends and acquaintances who were the product of broken homes. Their parents may or may not have been present for their children and they often let them fall through the cracks. She had been hopelessly spoiled, not with material items but praise. As an only child, her parents doted on her. She was told there were no limitations on what she could do. She never let them down and was a model child beyond the occasional rebellion or disrespectful attitude when she had to be denied something they could not afford. But those were behaviors consistent with growing up. If loving her too much was her parents' worst mistake, she knew she had a blessed life.

Her initial exhilaration on opening the acceptance letter to Harvard had quickly faded. She felt woefully inadequate compared to the students and faculty she would meet and nearly passed up the opportunity to attend the Ivy League school because of those fears. It was her parents who reassured her she would not have been accepted had she not been worthy. It was her humble beginnings and hard work which gave her the opportunity, and she needed to grasp all it offered.

Her parents had been right. She met many students from similar backgrounds who, like Laurel, had scholarships. It was the students from the privileged families which most intimidated her. If she could not compete financially, she would academically. She threw herself into the academics only and sadly neglected tempering it with a social life. The result was a highly educated and dependable young woman who was largely naïve in the social areas of her life. When she first met Chaz, she had recently returned from Europe where she had furthered her education and work experience. Little had changed socially, but once in Manhattan, poised for success, she was ready for romance and vulnerable.

He was both charming and intriguing. Chaz had many attributes and failings. His one failing had not been his devotion to Laurel. He was genuine in his love for her, but his ambition was his Achilles heel. He had not had the good fortune of having a stable home. He had been of those children who *fell through the cracks*. He seldom spoke of his childhood, but when he did, Laurel had the impression it left him with an inferiority complex. He had the constant need to prove himself. She had no way of knowing his biggest regret was letting her down. He could rationalize what he did to his clients with thoughts of *they were greedy and wanted a quick return* or *they could afford to take risks*. He could not say that about Laurel, she was his partner and his heart, and he destroyed that with his recklessness. He ran away as much to avoid facing her as he did to face the law. Laurel began to understand that but could not justify it.

She may not have been through psychoanalyzing herself, but she was done with mowing the lawn. She climbed off the mower, brushed the grass clippings from her clothes, and examined her work. It looked terrible. She had let it go too long without tending to it, and she realized she would have to cut it a couple more times to make it presentable. She certainly had the time to do it, but she wanted instant gratification.

Over the course of the next couple of weeks, she did little else but mow, trim, clip, weed, and think. The lawn looked great; she only wished the inside of her head equaled it. Eventually she would have to make a life plan. She hated how much she missed Chaz and wondered if he felt the same way. It was best she never knew he did; that was a ship which had sailed.

When she was the president of the Bridgefield Bank, she had been involved in various charitable causes. The corporate office insisted local branches reach out to the community, support local interests, and needs. It was one of the things she had enjoyed the most in her position. The bank had a designated account for her to use at her discretion. She took part in health-related walk-a-thons, basket raffles, and spaghetti dinners.

The events which touched her personally were the ones involving children. It broke her heart to see a child ill. She wanted to volunteer again, but she was not ready. She needed to let the dust settle around her scandal. She wanted to be trusted, and she feared lingering doubt among her acquaintances. There would always be people who gossiped, preferring to believe the worst, but few had a negative opinion of her and that fact would present itself to her.

One afternoon, while she was in the backyard, she noticed a beautiful pink bloom on her mother's rosebush. She decided to clip it, put it in a bud vase and set it on her parents' headstone. She had not returned since the day she had struck her head.

She drove up the winding lane closest to their grave and parked her car. She took particular care to watch her footing because she did not want a repeat of her last painful episode. She placed the vase on the flat base of the headstone and wished her mother could see the perfection of the rosebud. She suddenly felt an odd sense of peace and well-being. She wanted to believe it was because her mother did know.

She was startled when she heard a voice. "How's your head?"

Seeing the woman who had been there when she fell, Laurel smiled. "Better, but it sure hurt at the time."

"I bet it did. Did you go to the hospital?"

Laurel shook her head. "You won't believe it, but the doctor you mentioned happened to pass by and treated me."

The woman's face brightened. "And now for the rest of the story."

Laurel was amused by her match making attempt. "There is no story. He cleansed my wound, and we went our separate ways."

"There's still hope. It's pretty hilly in here and you could twist your ankle."

Now laughing, Laurel asked, "Are you trying to fix me up or kill me?"

The old woman made a grand gesture with both hands. "Look where we are, dear."

Laurel asked, "Where's the bathrobe and slippers?"

Today the woman wore a comfortable leisure suit. Pretending to be aghast she replied, "I can't be seen in the same thing every day."

"I thought you told me no one pays any attention to you." Laurel prodded her with good nature.

"They don't, but I do. My opinion of me is the only one that counts," she said with a wink, then added, "I must be going, maybe we'll run into each other again. Take care, dear."

She watched in admiration as the sweet old woman headed toward the road. She had touched on a nerve in Laurel. She had been too worried about what other people would think of her. If there was one thing which was holding her back it was that, but she was also not certain she wanted to get close to anyone. The two things were not necessarily mutually exclusive. The old woman seemed to know that. Either she was astute, or Laurel needed to read more into it.

She finished paying her respects to her parents and started to leave when she spotted the pond with a pair of swans swimming around. There was something hypnotizing about it, so she pulled off one of the lanes, parked her car, and walked over to it. It had been thoughtfully landscaped with ample benches for visitors to use. It really was a beautiful place. She could understand why it was a tourist attraction.

She'd lived nearby her entire childhood and never appreciated its charm. Until this moment she had thought of a cemetery only as a place of death. Now she saw it was just as much about life. She was contemplating that thought when an elderly caretaker drove up next to her on an electric golf cart.

He smiled as he reached for a bucket near his foot. "I like to feed them."

The swans instantly recognized him and quickly swam toward him. He tossed the pellets out into the pond where they gobbled them down. He offered her the bucket. "Would you like to feed them?"

"Thank you." She grabbed a handful of pellets, then asked, "Do you do this every day?"

He nodded. "Even when I'm not working. If I can't make it for some reason, my grandson does it for me. These are not domestic swans, you know. They migrate south in the fall, so I don't have to worry about them in the winter."

Laurel looked around the vast acreage. "Do you take care of this whole cemetery?"

"Good heavens, no. The cemetery association gives me a modest stipend. I just enjoy the beauty and history here. There are full-time lawn maintenance people and many volunteers just like me. There are even guided tours available by appointment."

Shaking her head, she said, "I had no idea."

"There are a lot of stories here. People find themselves lost and are drawn to the cemetery where their loved ones rest. I see them praying, crying, laughing, and sometimes even cursing as they stand over a headstone. Everyone has a journey and purpose, and this place is a serene reminder of that."

She sighed. "I wish they could share that journey with me."

"They do if you look for it."

She waited for a ghost story or something of that nature, but he said, "Take a look at some of the headstones. There is more information on them than you might expect. They list the wars they fought all the way back to pre-revolutionary days. Names of spouses and children, how long they were on this earth, and sometimes how they died. You'll learn how they lived through epidemics, losing children, and still striving to create the next generation. They aren't just a name and date etched in stone."

"No, no, they're not." She thought of her parents and other relatives.

"I've bored you long enough with my stories. Good day to you, miss." He then disappeared down a lane in his golf cart.

She was beginning to feel foolish. Even the

troubles she was experiencing were manageable with a little courage and a thicker skin. She realized it was the first time she had not been protected from failure. She had setbacks, as everyone had, but no real failures until now. She considered what advice her parents would give her. Her mother once told her, "You always know where you want to go, but sometimes not how to get there." That was how she felt now.

She needed to find her passion. She had neglected that in the past because she'd she was either been studying or working. She and Chaz took vacations but never had any real hobbies or outside interests. A solution to that problem would present itself.

Laurel was puttering in the yard when a car pulled into her driveway. She'd had no visitors since her move to Rose Hill, apart from an occasional neighbor stopping by briefly as they were passing. She did not recognize the car, but she was familiar with its occupant as he stepped out of the vehicle.

"Mr. Prentice, what on earth are you doing out here?" she asked with genuine surprise.

Donald Prentice was the founder of the Children's Leukemia Foundation in the nearby city of Buffalo. She had taken part in fundraising during her tenure at the bank.

"After a bit of poking around, I tracked you down. Do you have a few minutes for me?"

A little flustered, still reeling from her recent disgrace, she answered, "Certainly, please come inside."

She ushered him to the living room and offered him a chair as she sat opposite of him. "Can I get you something, maybe coffee or tea?"

He waved his hand. "Thank you, no. I'll get to the point; I want your help with this years' fundraiser. Our person who normally is in charge had a family emergency and had to take an indefinite leave."

Mr. Prentice's sudden appearance at her door, coupled with a request for her help, left her unsettled. She wondered what he may have known about her recent departure from the bank. She needed to momentarily distract herself while she regrouped. She ignored his response to an offer of refreshments and excused herself to the kitchen. She prepared a tray of cookies and iced tea. She nearly dropped a glass, catching it at the last minute but not before knocking the cookie tin to the floor causing a loud crash.

"Is everything all right?" he asked. "Can I give you a hand?"

Bringing the tray to the living room, she set it before him. She stared at it instead of looking him in the eyes. She hesitated before stating, "I'm flattered you would ask for my help, but do you know I am no longer at the bank?"

He nodded. "I'm aware of that and also of the events which precipitated your leaving. I know you were completely exonerated of any wrongdoing."

"Nevertheless, I'm not certain I would be your best choice. Appearances matter in fundraising."

"Don't you want to take the position? You would be paid a salary, not what you made at the bank, but it's significant."

She was compelled to point out the obvious. "Don, you're not just talking about this one fundraiser; you need someone full time? It's not that I don't want to accept. I think it's an important cause, too important for me to taint your efforts to raise money."

"If I thought you would risk our fundraising efforts or management of the trust, I wouldn't be here," he countered. "You underestimate the respect people have for you."

"Are you sure of that? I am prepared to handle any insults or disparaging comments concerning my character. I'm not prepared to do it at the expense of the Children's Leukemia Foundation."

"Let me worry about that. You would be primarily working behind the scenes. The annual event and daily operations require someone with organizational skills and fiscal knowledge. That person is you."

"There are several people you could have asked. Why did you ask me?"

"You're right; there were others I could have asked; I appreciate your reticence," he admitted. "You have something we really need and that's heart. The people I would ask if you turned me down would take the job, but that's exactly what it would be for them, a job. I want more than that."

"Can I give it some thought?"

His tone became more somber. "Of course, but I want to tell you one thing first. Janet Miller's daughter has just been diagnosed with leukemia.

Sickened by the news, it felt like she'd been punched in the stomach. Janet, the head teller at the bank, was the person she had been most personally connected with. They often dined together with their husbands; the Millers had been guests at her Bridgefield home for picnics and parties. Janet had reached out to her many times in the past months, but Laurel was never able to bring herself to speak with her.

"I can't believe I've been so self-absorbed I didn't know. She was probably afraid to burden me. Will her daughter be okay?"

Shaking his head, Don replied, "She has only been recently diagnosed. You've been involved with us in the past, so I know you are familiar with the process."

"I know there are many treatment options, including bone marrow transplants."

"As far as I know, it hasn't gotten to that yet. Even if you don't take the position, I think you should reach out to Janet. She, like you, needs a friend right now."

Laurel gave him a suspicious look. "You play dirty. You knew my heart would break for her."

"I make no apologies for that. Leukemia is a dirty disease."

"Nevertheless, can you give me a couple of days?"

"Of course, I'll send over a job description with all the usual expectations and requirements. I have no doubt you will understand why we need you."

After he left, she nearly cried. Janet Miller had tried to contact her at least a half a dozen times, and she ignored her attempts to be a good friend. She feared Janet may do the same thing to her, but she'd have to take that risk. A child with a life-threatening illness took precedence over her own problems. She needed to make amends and help in any manner she could. It was circumstances like these that changed a person's priorities.

Chapter Six

Over the course of a couple of days, Laurel must have picked up her phone half a dozen times to call Janet. Each time she hung up before it could ring. She did not know what to say to her. It became even more difficult after the information from Don Prentice arrived. She pored over it and a tear dripped down her cheek as she thought of Janet's daughter, Missy.

It may have seemed ironic she would seek out the cemetery to sort out her thoughts about how to approach Janet. She was sitting on the bench near the pond when her eccentric cemetery friend sat down next to her. Subconsciously, she was looking for some guidance and inspiration and was grateful for her presence.

"You look deep in thought."

Turning to her Laurel replied, "I just found out a dear friend's daughter is seriously ill."

"I'm so sorry. How is she taking it?"

Head bowed in shame, Laurel responded, "That's just it; I don't know. I've been afraid to call her."

"If you're friends, then why are you afraid to contact her?"

Lifting her head, she looked into the old woman's compassionate eyes. "I've been caught up in my own problems and distanced myself from her and others, even when they tried to help me. I guess I thought if I can't help myself, what use am I to anyone else."

The old woman nodded. "I could see where that might give you pause to call her, but saying nothing is worse. If she rebuffs you, that's on her."

"You're right. Why is it easier to shoulder your own problems than those of people you care about?"

"Sadly, not too many people can say that. You obviously are a person of great compassion. Do you want my advice? I'd probably give it to you anyway."

As Laurel detected a hint of a smile on her face she murmured, "Please."

"Don't call her; show up in person. It will take more courage, but there is nothing like a face-to-face meeting to gauge a person's feelings. Anyone can make a phone call or send a text message—in person is the only real test."

"I think you're right. I needed someone to tell me that. If the worst happened and I never let Janet know how much she and her family meant to me, I'd never forgive myself."

"I'm long on opinions, not always correct, but I've got them," the woman said with humor.

Laurel stood up and replied, "I guess I had better do this now while I have the courage. Thank you."

"You're welcome, and I hope things work out."

****

It was a short drive to Janet's Bridgefield home, a drive she should have taken when she first learned the devastating news. Laurel was not certain she would find anyone at home, but she thought she would check there first. She took a deep breath before she rang the doorbell. She soon found herself staring face-to-face with her friend. Janet silently opened the door wide enough for Laurel to enter where they embraced, never uttering a word. When they separated, each had tears running down their cheeks.

All of Laurel's emotions bubbled to the surface before she spoke. "I just found out about Missy. I'm so sorry. I'm so sorry for a lot of things."

"You don't have to explain," Janet replied in a sympathetic tone. "I would have locked myself away too. I just didn't want you to think you were alone."

Between sniffles Laurel said, "I don't want you to think that either. I'm here for whatever you need."

"Who told you?" Janet asked.

"Don Prentice. He wants me come work for the foundation."

"You'd be perfect for the job."

"I needed to see you first before I made my final decision."

Janet was about to speak when Laurel heard her name being called. Missy ran into the room and threw her arms around her neck. "I've missed you. Where have you been?"

"Laurel had some important business to take care of, honey," her mother said. "I'm hoping that's done now."

"It is," Laurel said. "All over—you'll be seeing more of me now."

"I've been sick," the little girl said, more as a matter of being informative than to complain.

"I know. I'm certain the doctors will fix you up."

"That's what Mommy and Daddy tell me," she responded, innocent of what was likely to come.

Janet looked lovingly at her daughter. "Mommy and Laurel want to catch up. Why don't you go into the family room and play?"

"Can I watch cartoons?" she asked eagerly.

"Absolutely."

Laurel watched the energetic child run through the house. "You'd never know she was sick."

"There are good days and bad. The bad are only going to get worse. They are going to start her on chemotherapy soon."

Recent research into leukemia told Laurel enough to know what would come next. It would take all of Janet and her husband's resolve to get through it. "Are you still working at the bank?"

"I took an indefinite leave of absence. I want to spend as much time with Missy as I can. Our son is going to need attention too. He's too young to fully understand why so much attention is being given to Missy. I'm lucky I have in-laws nearby who are picking up the slack."

"I'm sure that must be a comfort to you. Typically, children love being spoiled by their grandparents. Where he may think it seems like you're giving Missy too much attention, he's getting it from them. It will be a balancing act for a while, but eventually he'll understand. You'll see, it will work out."

Janet took Laurel's hand and gave it a squeeze. "Take the job. Anything anyone can do to eradicate this awful illness has to be tried. It might not help Missy, but new treatments come out all the time. The Leukemia Society needs every dime. You have a lot to offer, or Mr. Prentice wouldn't have asked you to work with him."

She could see the pain in her friend's eyes. "I'll do what I can."

Laurel did not want to overstay her welcome, so she left stating, "Call me for anything. I can babysit, run errands, or simply sit and commiserate with you."

"If you take the job, that will be enough. I'll keep you informed, and maybe we can get together for lunch or something."

Laurel hugged her. "I'd like that."

She went directly home and re-read the information Don Prentice had sent her. The Children's Leukemia Foundation was a local charity in which the money raised was used at the Children's Hospital in the city. It did donate money toward research on the national level, but it was primarily for the benefit of local children. They bought new and improved equipment and contributed to temporary housing for parents with children in treatment.

Under the guiding hand of Don Prentice, the foundation's trust fund grew to a multi-million-dollar investment. He told Laurel there was a reason he sought her out. He went on to say he was getting on in years and was hoping to groom someone to eventually replace him. She had everything he needed, and he suspected she needed something to do. Even if she found a more lucrative position, more in keeping with her education and experience, he was certain she would at least remain involved. It didn't take long to realize his intentions; Don Prentice was not subtle.

In the same packet he sent her, there were dozens of pictures of children who had successfully undergone treatment at the hospital. He attached a post-it sticker in his handwriting saying, "You can help us save more."

Shaking her head and smiling, she said, "You win." She then called him and said she would take the position. Most of her work could be done remotely from home, but she would have an office in the city at their headquarters. Not one to do things halfway she threw all her energy into her job. She found it was entirely different managing the foundation, versus volunteering to help at events.

She was still uncomfortable and even insecure about her recent humiliation. Don Prentice was sensitive to that and helped to shield her from dealing with too many people. He assigned one of their long-time employees to be her personal assistant and act as a go between with public events. Laurel wasn't being cowardly; she just did not want to be a negative influence on such a stellar charity. Professional meetings were not a problem. She regularly had conferences or luncheons with various professionals and corporation heads. It was essential to be engaged both for informational purposes as well as financial.

****

After familiarizing herself with the intricacies of her new job, Laurel wanted to gather as many professionals together as possible. A group of local pediatric oncologists were invited for an informal luncheon catered at her office. As Mr. Prentice said he wanted feedback from them on new acquisitions of medical equipment, he thought it would be an excellent opportunity for Laurel to get to know the doctors they had been helping.

"I have an acceptance from fifteen doctors," her assistant Connie informed her.

"Fifteen? I didn't know there were that many pediatric oncologists at the hospital," Laurel said.

Connie explained the reason for so many attendees.

"There aren't, but other doctors attend too if their field of medicine warrants it."

"I'll make sure we have enough folders for everyone. I've outlined the budget we must work with and a questionnaire for them to fill out on what they would like to see us help them acquire."

When Laurel entered the conference room, the doctors were milling around conversing with one another. "Good afternoon, everyone. Thank you for attending today. I'm Laurel Quincy, the new director of financial acquisitions. I hope to get to know each one of you personally."

A familiar voice called out from the group. "Everyone?"

"Even Dr. Bradford." Clarifying her response, she said, "He and I met in Pioneer Cemetery after I fell and cracked my head open. Fortunately, I didn't hurt anything that mattered."

Everyone laughed, and she continued with the meeting. She received some constructive feedback which she hoped would be beneficial. It was one thing to theorize and another to have doctors who were on the frontlines at the hospital. One of the doctors approached her at the end of the meeting. "Nothing against your predecessor—he was a great guy—but you are more suited to this position. I'm looking forward to working with you."

"Thank you, this has become personal. A little girl I am very fond of has recently been diagnosed with leukemia."

"That does give one an incentive," he said. "Is she local?"

"Her name is Missy Miller. I'm certain you will be

seeing her."

He nodded but did not confirm her statement. Laurel assumed he may have already been consulted, but it would violate confidentiality to admit that.

After the luncheon was over, she gathered her files, dodging the clean-up crew who noisily clanged dishes and dragged garbage cans across the floor. She had been so preoccupied with her presentation, she was the only one who had not eaten. Laurel impulsively grabbed the last slice of cake before it was tossed out with the rest of the garbage. She was shoving it into her mouth when a straggler from the meeting spoke to her.

"You were just about the last person I expected to see here today," Dr. Bradford told her.

She was pleased to see a familiar face but embarrassed she had been caught with a mouth full of cake. She tried to quickly swallow, but it got caught in her throat and she started coughing. "I wasn't expecting you either. I didn't know you were a pediatric oncologist."

He smiled as he pointed to a spot on her face with the cake frosting. "I'm not, but I have had a few cases in my career. I attend meetings like this on different illnesses which may affect my patients. The first doctor to see them is generally the pediatrician or a primary doctor. The sooner we recognize a potential problem the better able we are to have them treated. I also try to stay on top of diabetes cases. I see more of them than I do cancer."

As he spoke, Laurel reached for a napkin off the catering cart to wipe her face and then discreetly tucked it in her pocket. "No disease is ever welcome, but I suppose that's good."

He shrugged. "Yes and no. Diabetes can be managed but not cured; cancers are harder on the patient, but they can be cured in many instances. Research has come a long way in leukemia cases."

"Yes, and that's why I am committed to organizations like this one that raise money and awareness."

"You haven't been here long, have you?"

With a shake of her head, she said, "I literally just started. I used to volunteer for their fundraising events and when a position opened, Mr. Prentice asked me to join the foundation. I was in between jobs so I accepted."

"What kind of work were you in?"

She tried not to sound nervous about answering. "Finance. I have an MBA from Harvard."

He was impressed and said so. "They are lucky to have someone so qualified."

"The timing was right and seemed like a good fit."

He changed the subject to her recent injury. "It looks like your head healed up. May I?" he asked indicating he wanted to check her head.

She pulled back a lock of hair and showed him a slight scar.

As he ran his finger over the healed gash, she felt the warmth of his touch. "That'll go away in a few months; it's hardly even noticeable now."

She gave a dismissive wave. "I'm not planning on entering any beauty pageants."

"The pageant's loss. But as to why I'm here. As a supporter of the Children's Hospital, we're lucky to have it so close and any money raised for it is well deserved. Does the foundation support other groups?"

"No, we strictly concentrate on leukemia; however, any equipment or outreach services related to the hospital are readily shared."

"I'm glad to hear that. My mother sponsored a hospitality house for relatives of patients. It was dear to her heart because my little brother spent many months at the hospital. We lived close enough to drive back and forth, but she often met families who did not have that luxury."

"I'm so sorry. If you don't mind me asking, what was wrong with your brother?"

"He had a congenital heart defect and required a dozen surgeries before he was two years old."

Because he answered in an informational tone, not one of remorse, she felt it was safe to ask, "And where is he now?"

"Boston. He is the station manager for the local public broadcasting affiliate. Too highbrow for me."

"Somehow, I doubt that. Your parents must be proud of their sons."

"They were. They are both gone."

"I know that feeling. I wish I would have had a sibling to share my memories with, but I'm certain they felt they couldn't improve upon perfection."

He nodded in agreement. "I'm sure you're right."

Laurel was enjoying their impromptu conversation. She had been so uptight and out of sorts with her life she had nearly forgotten how to relax. She sensed he liked talking to her too because sought her out after the meeting.

"Did you get your lawnmower running?"

She brightened. "I did. I think if this fundraising thing doesn't work out for me, I'll open a repair shop."

He looked at her hands with their perfectly manicured nails. "I don't think you should push your luck."

She shrugged. "I think you're right."

He glanced at his watch. "Damn, I'm late for my afternoon appointments. I have a receptionist who runs my office like a drill sergeant. Is there any chance I could take you to dinner some night?"

Before she could respond, his cellphone rang. Laurel smiled when she heard a woman cussing him out for leaving her with a waiting room full of patients.

He gave her a defeated gesture and mouthed the words, "I'll call you," before he darted out of the room.

Laurel was not certain how she would have answered him. She did not want to date, but she knew she could use some companionship. She had been living at her parent's house for months and barely left except for necessities and now for her job. She was also being selfish by hoping he may be able to give her some valuable insight into making the foundation more efficient.

She did not want to approach her position from a monetary position only. It was important that she never lose sight of the individuals they were helping. It was the photos in the informational packet that Don Prentice had given her which swayed her toward accepting the job. That fact coupled with Missy's illness made her job personal. Dr. Bradford may even be able to make her a better friend to Janet during the troubling times she had ahead of her. She would wait to hear from him before deciding what she wanted to do.

When she went back into her office, Don Prentice was waiting. "I heard you had a productive meeting."

"I don't know that I would say productive; we were going over some future plans and wish lists. I'm still trying to feel my way around."

"You impressed Dr. Norman."

"I'm happy he was pleased, but what does that have to do with the success of the meeting?" she asked.

"I probably should have told you this before, but he is not associated with the hospital. He is world renowned for his research, and we have been trying to bring him on board as a consultant, both for the foundation and the hospital. He has enormous clout in the research arena. He is exactly the kind of professional you want on speed dial."

"I'll make a point of keeping him informed of our fundraising and acquisitions for the hospital. Even if he doesn't consult with us, he may like to know what we're doing."

Don gave her a mischievous wink. "I'm counting on that."

Chapter Seven

Laurel was driving home from the city after the meeting with the doctors. She wasn't entirely certain why the thought occurred to her, but she remembered there was a feed store on her route. She pulled into the parking lot of the large warehouse and went inside. There was every type of animal feed imaginable. Once outside of the city, there were cattle and horse farms dotting the countryside. It was the only feed store in the area, making it a staple for anyone needing supplies. She felt completely out of place. She did not know the first thing about the various feeds. As a child, her only pet had been an orange tabby cat. Her ignorance must have shown because a young man approached her and asked if he could be of help.

"What kind of feed would you give swans?"

He told her there were many people in the area who raised waterfowl, so it was not an unusual request. "You raise swans?"

"No, I want to feed the ones at Pioneer Cemetery."

He smiled. "You and dozens of other people."

She thought she was unique in her desire to both entertain herself and do a good deed and kept thinking about the elderly caretaker who fed the birds each day with such devotion. They looked so regal as they approached the shore for their daily meal; she hoped they would eventually do the same thing for her.

After educating her on the various feeds with the pros and cons to each type, Laurel deferred to his judgment. The young man rang up her purchase, then placed the fifty-pound bag of feed in her trunk. "Trust me, they aren't starving. Just take a bucketful with you each time you go and toss it to them."

She thanked him and when she returned home, lugged the bag into the corner of her garage where she would fill a bucket in the morning to feed them. She wanted to go early to be there ahead of any work crews.

The following morning was sunny and dry with the air fragrant from her mother's rosebushes. She stopped to admire them before heading for her car. She did not have to go into the city and could work from home, so she had plenty of time to spoil the swans. She drove directly to the pond and the bench closest to it but found it occupied.

Initially, she was annoyed. She'd simply wanted a few moments alone to commune with the wildlife. When she grabbed the bucket of feed and walked toward the bench, she was happy to see it was her elderly friend who seemed to be lost in reverie.

"Hello," Laurel said.

The elderly woman looked up. "Good to see you. What do you have with you?"

"Food for the swans and whatever birds might want it."

"They'll appreciate it. They kept looking at me like I was some kind of a freeloader."

Laurel walked to the edge of the tranquil pond and tossed a handful of pellets onto the water. Reluctantly the swans and a couple of ducks headed her way. She looked over at the woman. "They don't trust me."

She giggled. "They only really trust Harold."

"Is he the caretaker?"

She nodded. "I call him the fowl whisperer."

Laurel laughed aloud. "I'm not certain that sounds like a compliment."

"Ah, he can take it."

Laurel looked at her new friend. "Why are you wearing the pink slippers but not your bathrobe?"

The old woman looked down and flexed her toes. "Because they are so comfortable. I hate to break up the ensemble, but they'll get over it."

Laurel sat next to her, then said in a serious tone, "I need to thank you."

The woman looked at her intently. "For what?"

"I told you about my friend having a sick child."

The woman nodded.

"I took your advice, and I went to visit her in person."

"And?"

"You were absolutely right; we needed to meet face-to-face."

"There is little substitute for that."

"I've taken a job where I may be able to help children just like my friend's daughter."

"I'd call that an all-around win."

"I sure hope you're right. By the way, I've never asked your name."

"I'm Maggie, and yours?"

"Laurel."

"It's a pleasure. My family gets a little sick of listening to me, so it's been nice knowing I might have helped someone."

"It was greatly appreciated. This was the kind of

thing I would have taken to my mother. I'm pretty sure she would have given me the same advice."

"Then you already knew the right thing to do."

Laurel looked at her and was silent for a moment while she thought about it. "You're right again. I guess I needed someone else to tell me that."

"You know," Maggie started, sounding sheepish, "That cute doctor usually jogs by here about this time."

Laurel laughed. "Do you have a one-track mind?"

"Pretty much. It's not like I'm likely to get myself a boyfriend."

Laurel smiled at the irascible woman as Maggie gave her a salute and headed in the direction of the development. Laurel kept tossing pellets to the birds, after a few minutes they were not the least bit reluctant to swim toward her.

Just as Maggie predicted, David approached the pond wearing jogging shorts and a T-shirt. He was pleasantly surprised to see her. "Hi."

"Good morning. Do you run here every day?"

He motioned to the bench for permission to join her and sat down.

"Weather permitting, I like running here, but I'm not a fanatic about it. It doesn't get better than today with the sun shining and the birds singing."

"How did you get started coming here of all places?"

"One of my colleagues suggested it. When I was trying to get a handle on my stress, he recommended I start jogging here. He said it was much safer than the roadways, and there are no bike paths nearby to safely jog. The hilly terrain makes it more challenging. He was also a little worried about me and knew there was enough foot traffic here if something happened. He made it sound like I might need a defibrillator. Doctors can be so dramatic."

She commented with humor. "You mean like falling and cracking your head like I did."

He nodded. "You meet really nice people here. They all seem to be looking for the same sense of peace while getting some exercise, at least the ones I've spoken with say that."

"I just like clearing my head, and I've been drawn to the pond. Are there any fish in it?"

"Some bass and a few carp. I see kids here fishing with their grandparents from time to time."

"How long does it take for your entire run?"

"If I go up and down each road and I'm having a good day, it takes me about an hour. When I first started, I was so out of shape both physically and mentally I ran about a quarter of a mile and collapsed. If it hadn't been for some lady, I probably would still be there."

Laurel's curiosity was piqued when he mentioned that. "Was she a small, elderly woman with white hair who may or may not have been wearing a bathrobe and slippers?"

He looked at her like she was crazy. "You met a woman dressed like that? I've seen some, shall we say, very casual wear, but not a bathrobe and slippers."

Laurel started laughing. "She lives in that development off the north end. She found me when I first fell. In fact, she was the one who told me a doctor runs through here. She is quite the character, and I look forward to seeing her."

Smiling he nodded. "So that's why you knew I was

a doctor. I don't recall speaking with her, but there are so many people who take their walks here, usually with a dog on a leash."

"She has a wonderful sense of humor and a quick comeback. She gave me some good advice lately about helping a friend."

"When you aren't personally involved, it's easier to dispense advice. I had a similar experience with the woman who helped me."

"How so?"

He hesitated before answering, indicating to her he may not want to go into intimate details. He was brief. "I was engaged to be married and was left at the altar."

"Does that really happen? I thought that was for dramatic effect in movies."

"I am being dramatic, but it was nearly true. Two days before the wedding she called it off. She said she just couldn't see herself being tied down to a workaholic. At least, that's the excuse she gave."

"I assume there was some truth to that?" Laurel asked, remembering a little about what he had previously told her.

He shrugged. "Only partially, I didn't really become a workaholic until she left me. I found out she was having an affair with her boss. They are now married with a baby."

"Ouch."

"Exactly. When I started running here, everything caught up to me, and for a lack of a better word, I had a breakdown. I sat on the ground and started crying. That's when this older lady came along and sat down on the ground next to me and said absolutely nothing. When I finally looked up, she asked, 'Do you want to talk about it?' I've never done this before, but I poured my heart out to her."

"Must be something about this place which brings out the motherly instincts in people." Laurel started smiling thinking about Maggie and her direct approach to life. "Was she as opinionated as the woman I told you about?"

"No, not at all. When I finished my tale of woe she asked, 'What are you going to do about it?' I realized I had no answer and told her that, she then added, 'Then I'll find you lying in this same spot tomorrow. You can move forward or lie still. Which do you prefer?' It was like a proverbial slap in my face. I knew I couldn't stay like that, so every day I ran a little farther and my mind became a little clearer. I'm okay now, but it took an outsider to help me get there."

"Do you still see the woman who helped you?"

"Occasionally, usually we wave in passing. She seems like an incredibly quiet, thoughtful person who wouldn't want to risk embarrassing me. I'm beyond that now," he answered, then added,"I suspect you have a similar story. Am I wrong?"

She was reluctant to bare her soul and stated as much. She kept her answer brief. "I'm not at your healing point yet. Let's just say it would have been better if I had been left at the altar."

He put his hand on her shoulder in an understanding gesture. "Honestly, I wasn't prying."

She felt the compassion in his touch and answered. "I know that."

"I'd still like to take you to dinner. There are a lot of questions I'd like to ask you about your work. Would Saturday work for you?"

She wasn't sure she was ready to accept what she perceived to be a date, but found herself saying, "Sure."

"Great, I'll pick you up at seven."

She nodded. "I have your number from your card, but I don't think you have mine. I'll text it to you in case you get an emergency or something, then you can call me."

"It's not my week on call, but I should have your number."

Laurel worked for a while at home and then decided to stop by the bakery in the village to pick up some cupcakes to take to Janet's house. They had been calling each other regularly, but she did not make a point of dropping in on her unannounced. She was never certain if the family was up to visitors. She didn't want to put her friend in a position where she had to be polite when she really wanted privacy. Placing the box on the seat next to her, she phoned Janet and tried to sound as upbeat as possible. "Are you up for some cupcakes?"

"Missy is napping, my son is with his grandparents, and my husband is working. He tries to get in as many hours as possible. We need the extra money with me being on a leave of absence, and there will undoubtedly be days he'll have to take time off. In other words, I could use the company."

"I'll be right there."

A few minutes later, she was at Janet's door. She handed her the box as she stepped into her friend's front hallway. "Are the cupcakes a bad idea? I didn't know if Missy was well enough to eat them. I wanted to bring something."

"She'll love them. They haven't started chemo yet.

They are currently trying to boost her immune system."

Laurel's heart went out to Janet, giving her a hug. "I dissect every bit of information that comes across my desk, hoping to help Missy."

Gratitude sounded in Janet's voice. "I'm so proud of you for taking the position.

"Proud? Why would that make you proud of me?"

"You have been dealt a heavy blow with Chaz's downfall and betrayal of your trust. Your career was, maybe not destroyed, but certainly sidelined through no fault of your own. It takes a strong person to bounce back."

"I wouldn't say through no fault of my own. I should have recognized the signs he was up to something. That never would have happened to me at the bank. I would have caught it at once."

Clearly, Janet did not agree. "The circumstances were different. In any event, I know it's hard for you to put yourself back out in the business world."

"It was less traumatic than I expected. Mr. Prentice has made it possible for me to work at home as well as at the office, and my contacts are usually other employees. I did have an informational meeting with some of the oncologists and a few other doctors. I'm happy with keeping everything low key. I realize I'm a little paranoid and think everyone is talking about me."

"That's only natural; you're old news now," Janet said. "It's been months since Chaz disappeared. There are new things for people to talk about."

Laurel laughed nervously. "You're a good friend, but you know as well as I do, Bridgefield is a small town, and my rapid departure is probably still discussed."

"Let them talk; we know differently. There are petty and insecure people out there that would try to alleviate their own failings by talking about yours; don't let that happen. It may not seem like it now, but staying the course as you always have is what will carry you through. Time will be your friend."

"I don't see that I have much choice," she answered, then said, "I came to cheer you up, not the other way around."

Janet reached into the box and pulled out a cupcake. "Any distraction right now is exactly what I need. I can throw my opinions and advice toward you because I can; curing Missy, I can't."

Laurel had a mischievous gleam in her eye. "In that case, what would you say if I told you I have a date on Saturday?"

Janet was so surprised she nearly spit out her cupcake. "You? A date?"

Pretending to be offended Laurel, said, "Do you think no one would want to go out with me?"

Janet giggled. "I'm sure someone would. I just didn't think you were ready. I know the kind of person you are, and opening yourself to a new relationship must be difficult. You and Chaz were inseparable."

With the same sarcastic tone Laurel, said, "And we saw how that worked out. Maybe I'm not ready, but I have an ulterior motive. He's a pediatrician who had attended my meeting, and I thought I might learn something from him to help Missy. He is quite dedicated to his patients."

Janet grinned. "You picked up a doctor during a conference. He must be easy."

"Get your mind out of the gutter. I met him weeks

ago in Pioneer Cemetery."

Janet tried unsuccessfully not to laugh. "This story doesn't get any better. You had to meet someone in a cemetery?"

Laughing, Laurel agreed. "It does sound weird, but it was just one of those happenstance things. He, like dozens of others, jogs on the driveways. I had fallen and struck my head, and he helped me out. We have bumped into each other a couple of times since then. When he was at the meeting, we talked and again at the cemetery. He asked me to dinner. Surprisingly, I accepted."

"Good for you. There is nothing to be gained sitting alone night after night. Who is this knight in shining armor?"

"David Bradford."

First, Janet's face went blank, then her eyes softened. "Put on something especially nice. Wear your best perfume. And keep him happy. I owe him."

"Is he the kids' pediatrician?"

Janet nodded. "Missy wasn't feeling well. The first stages of leukemia can be overlooked because it mimics several childhood illnesses. She was tired, running a fever, everything you associate with a cold or flu. He thought the same thing, but when she didn't get better, he was immediately suspicious of leukemia. He didn't tell us until after he had run some tests. The day he broke the news to us, he cried nearly as hard as us."

Laurel said, "That sounds like him. He told me he tries to keep abreast of illnesses because timing can make a difference. I don't doubt Missy is in capable hands."

"We've been taking the kids to him ever since he

started his practice. He's an exceptionally good doctor. He never tries to rush you out the door and takes his time building a relationship with the kids. Missy adores and trusts him. It's important for kids to trust their doctor, especially in her case when she is going through so many invasive tests."

Laurel quipped, "Well, at least you're pimping me out for a worthy cause."

Chapter Eight

When Saturday arrived, Laurel found herself nervous. She almost called David with an excuse not to see him. She hadn't been on a date in years; even before she started seeing Chaz, she had dated little. Her education and career had been more important.

She looked through her closet, taking out various dresses and pantsuits. She wished she had thought to ask where they were going, it would have given her a fashion hint. If there was one thing she had, it was an extensive wardrobe. As a bank executive she had conservative suits, but often an important part of her job was socializing. She had everything from evening gowns to sportswear for company picnics. She tried on one outfit after another saying to herself, "Too businesslike, too revealing, not revealing enough, or too casual." She eventually chose dress slacks and a silk blouse; they were right for almost any dining experience.

She started rummaging in her jewelry box for accessories when she spotted her wedding rings. She was gripped with an emotion somewhere between nostalgia and full-fledged anger. There was even a part of her which still felt married and she was cheating on her husband. It was ridiculous of course; nevertheless it crossed her mind. She took the rings, put them in a small box, and stashed them in the back of her dresser so she wouldn't have to look at them. She would decide later what to do with them. She settled on simple pearl stud earrings and a sapphire ring which had belonged to her mother.

She passed by a photo of her mother and asked, "Do you approve?"

She wished it could have spoken to her. She really wanted to know what her mother would have said about her whole situation. She'd loved Chaz, and it was mutual. He had always been thoughtful and kind to his mother-in-law, probably because he had no relationship with his own mother. Laurel wondered if her mother had been a steadying influence on him. He did not become reckless until after her mother's death.

Though it seemed a bit farfetched, Laurel still tried to find a deeper cause for his behavior. She concluded no matter how much her mother cared for Chaz, she would want him to be held accountable. Her parents were long on forgiveness if it was deserved, but that did not exclude responsibility for what he had done.

A few minutes before seven, Laurel's doorbell rang. When she answered it, David stood before her with a bouquet of wildflowers. She reached out to take them. "They're absolutely beautiful but unnecessary."

"I believe it is the polite social convention."

She took the flowers gratefully. "I'm afraid it has been a while since I have dated so I'm not sure."

"That makes two of us."

She then ushered him into the kitchen where she found a vase for the flowers. She was digging through the cabinets for one while he was looking around the room. "This is a charming little cottage. It's what I expected I'd find."

She filled the vase with water and arranged the flowers as she asked, "Why is that?"

"I guess we all tend to size people up when we first meet them. It's human nature. It's not just about the way they dress or speak. It's an unnamed feeling. I have so many new people in and out of my office it has become second nature to me, especially with children. Some you can be silly and lighthearted with, and others are so terrified you must convince them you've got everything handled. That same thing applies to their parents."

"That must take a great deal of finesse. Children are what make parents' hearts beat, and when they suffer, everyone in the family suffers. I've learned that from Janet. I don't think I could ever possess your skill for balancing everyone's needs."

"I don't think I could agree with you," he said. "You strike me as an overly orderly person who likes simplicity to counteract chaos. When you work, you're all in, and when you relax, you want comfort without distraction to clear your head."

"How do you know I'm not a complete ditz?"

"The organization and thoroughness of your presentation the other day could not have been put together by a ditz. When I ran into you at the gas station, and you were trying to fix your lawnmower it told me that the basic things in life matter to you."

She did not know how to respond to that evaluation. It made her a little uncomfortable to know she was being assessed. David looked at his watch and said, "We had better get going before our reservations are given away."

Once in the car she asked, "Where are we going?"

"Autumn Hill Inn. Do you know it?"

Actually, she quite familiar with the place. They were renowned for serving only locally sourced organic produce and meats. She had dined there many times with Chaz and an occasional client. She was also instrumental, as the Bridgefield Bank president, in issuing the owner an expansion loan. Suddenly she wished David had chosen a different restaurant.

"Yes, the food is incredibly good. They even serve game hen."

"At least you're acquainted with it. I've always wanted to dine there but never got around to doing to it. Many of my colleagues rave about it."

The picturesque country inn was perfectly nestled on a quiet, rural plot of land surrounded by trees. The gardens were modest but pleasant. The inn had large wraparound porches for seasonal dining and both formal and informal inside dining rooms. There were only five guest suites, but it was the restaurant which was the heart of the business.

A hostess directed them to their table near a large bay window allowing them a spectacular view. It was nearly dusk, but they could clearly see the rolling hills dotted with crops for future harvest. It added to the ambiance.

David took the liberty of ordering a bottle of wine while they looked over the menu. They hadn't even discussed appetizers when a plate of seafood stuffed mushrooms was brought to their table.

"We didn't order these," he said.

Laurel knew who had sent them over. The dish was one of her favorites. The owner knew that and must have seen her in the dining room. She hoped it wouldn't present an awkward moment for David.

"They are compliments of Mr. Zander," the waitress told him as she placed the plate before them.

David looked a little confused, prompting Laurel to explain. "Mr. Zander is the owner, and he happens to know I particularly like them. I can send them back if you wish."

"No, of course not. They look delicious. You must have dined here a lot."

She did not want to explain, but she was left with little choice when Mr. Zander appeared at their table. "Mrs. Tanner, it's so good to see you again. It's been far too long."

Laurel kept her composure but secretly wanted to crawl beneath the table. "I've been extremely busy of late. I'd like to introduce you to my escort, Dr. David Bradford."

She prayed Mr. Zander would refrain from too much chitchat. He was a valued customer at the bank and naturally knew about Laurel's departure. At least she assumed someone would have told him. She had garnered the trust of several business owners, and they would most certainly have inquired about her. Making her customers have confidence with their banking needs had been her strength.

He made his greeting short. "It's a pleasure, Dr. Bradford. I hope you will become a regular."

Laurel was about to explain about being called Mrs. Tanner, but David reached across the table and placed his hand on top of hers. "I know who you are, and you don't owe me any explanations."

She was somewhat relieved that he knew. "Who told you?"

"No one was gossiping if that's what is concerning you. I thought you looked familiar, but it wasn't until after the conference I realized why. My practice has its business accounts at Bridgefield Savings and Loan. I had seen you from time to time but had no occasion to personally meet with you. The head teller handled all my accounts."

"How much do you know?"

Shaking his head, he said, "Only what I read in the paper. I know about your husband, or ex-husband. I also know you were cleared of any involvement. What I don't know is why the bank didn't keep you on. That seems unfair."

"Fair is relative. Maybe in the long run it was better that I do not try to repair the past but forge ahead with something new. Even if they had kept me on, I don't know if I could have overcome the stigma."

"You don't have to talk about it. Honestly, it's none of my business."

"It was just a matter of time before someone told you. This is a small community, and I knew a lot of people from the bank and when I helped in its expansion. It's disconcerting never knowing when something personal will pop up and embarrass me."

David sighed. "I know the feeling. I was completely humiliated when my fiancée dumped me right before the wedding. There were calls to guests and gifts to be returned, and the inevitable attempts for people to comfort me. They thought they were being kind when they cursed her, told me how horrible a person she was, etc. That made me feel worse because…"

Laurel interrupted him and said, "Because she was

the person you loved, and you didn't want to think how wrong you could have been."

"That sums it up. Was it that way with you too?"

She nodded. "Yes, but at least your fiancée didn't destroy dozens of people's lives, and your embarrassment wasn't played out in the local papers and television news."

"It still broke my heart."

"How long has it been?"

"Three years. You're the first woman I've asked for a date."

"Three years? I would have thought women would be throwing themselves at your feet." She wanted to add because he was a kind and handsome man but kept that thought to herself.

"No, I've been on many dates but never with someone I asked out of my own accord. I have some well-meaning friends who thought it was their duty to *fix me up*. There was never a second date."

Laurel smiled. "Their choice or yours?"

"If I'm honest, a little of both. I get the impression you haven't dated either."

"I was isolating myself until I could sort out my life. I didn't think it was fair to expose my baggage to anyone else. I'm not certain why I even accepted your invitation."

"It gets lonely, even when you are surrounded by people. All our friends know what had happened to us. You want to be close to someone with whom you can start out fresh. I don't know about you, but I don't want people telling me how I should be feeling. I try never to do that with others, especially considering my profession. People must deal with illnesses in their own way, and they can become incredibly angry at being told differently. Parents with seriously ill children are particularly volatile, and I can't blame them."

His statement brought her to another subject matter, Missy. "Since you mentioned that, a former co-worker and dear friend told me you are her daughter's pediatrician."

"Who is that?"

"Missy Miller."

From the look on his face, she knew he instantly recognized the name and the gravity of her condition. "I cannot confirm nor deny that; it would be a privacy issue for any doctor to tell someone else about a patient unless given express permission."

"Duly noted, but I'm not equally bound. I just want to tell you Janet is eternally grateful to you. She said if you hadn't been immediately suspicious of Missy's illness, it could have delayed diagnosis, using up valuable time. In fact, it was at Janet's urging that I accepted the position at the foundation. She wants me to help in any way I can to secure funding for research and treatments. I now understand what you meant when you told me you attend conferences to stay informed. It certainly has paid off for Missy and probably for other children under your care."

"That's very nice of you to say, but I'm not doing anything any competent doctor wouldn't do."

"That's the problem; there are too many incompetents out there. Maybe I'm being unkind in calling them incompetent, but uninformed is almost as bad."

He sighed. "There is nothing more gut-wrenching than watching a child suffer. I've had cases where I was sure I'd quit and find another profession, but then you save someone, and that child gets to grow up to live their life. You can't put a price on that."

She agreed. "No, you can't. My whole career has been about money and crunching numbers. It seems shamefully inconsequential."

"No money, no research. You are learning that now. People seem to forget there are a lot of cogs to make the world turn."

Neither was in a hurry to finish their dinner. They ate the appetizers Mr. Zander brought, sipped their wine through a dinner with a series of soup, salad, and the inn's specialty of Salmon Wellington. They savored each course without the conversation ever lagging. By the time dessert and coffee had been served, it was almost eleven o'clock. When Laurel looked around, she discovered the dining room was nearly empty, she looked at her watch.

"I've never taken this long to eat in my life."

"As a doctor, I can tell you it's best to eat slowly." He made it sound like a prescription.

"Slowly is an understatement. I think Mr. Zander is going to throw us out."

He stood up and helped her with her chair before leaving a very generous tip for their waitress. Laurel caught a glimpse of Mr. Zander, as he had watching them from the kitchen. She waved and mouthed the words, "Thank you."

Once in the car on the drive back to her house, she started yawning.

"Am I boring you?"

"I'm sorry, no you're not. I'm afraid all the food and wine are catching up to me."

"I'm in the same condition. At least, I have a short drive or I'd worry about falling asleep at the wheel."

He walked her to the door and leaned in to kiss her goodnight, but she surprised him by inviting him in. "Would some coffee keep you awake all night?"

He readily accepted. "After years of medical school, no coffee is strong enough to keep me awake."

She told him to make himself comfortable on the sofa while she prepared the coffee and a tray to bring it out to the living room. She sat next to him on the sofa and poured the rich brew into cups. Its aroma alone would keep her from sleeping, but she didn't care.

"I told you about my assumptions about you; what were yours about me?"

She thought for a moment while nervously biting her lip. "I intuitively knew you were a kind person to have stopped to help when I fell, but honestly, I was so sick to my stomach I just wanted to go home. Then again, at the gas station, you tried to help me with the lawnmower."

"You thought I was trying to hit on you?"

Sheepishly she replied, "Possibly, but I wasn't going to give you the chance. At that point, I hadn't been living in my home that long, and I was a mess."

"And now?"

She nervously tapped her fingers against her coffee cup. "Still a mess, but I think I have a direction to follow. It's unfortunate that it took the tragedy of Missy's illness for me to become motivated. My problems pale in comparison."

He nodded. "I was very young, but I can remember my mother saying something remarkably similar when my brother had all his heart surgeries. Later, when we were older, she never put an emphasis on things that didn't matter. I would go over to friends' homes and their parents were on their backs about picking up their clothes or taking out the trash, like it was the end of the world."

Laurel laughed. "Are you trying to say she let you be a slob?"

"Not by a long shot, but she wasn't going to make it ruin our day if those kinds of things didn't get done. What about your parents?"

She felt a little guilty when she told him, "It never came up, at least not often. I was an only child and, worse yet, a bookworm nerd. They understood I had different priorities, and I'm ashamed to say I never gave taking the trash out a single consideration. My mom worked part time at the drug store but was largely a stay-at-home parent. She seldom asked me to do anything."

"You said you mowed the lawn. You must have had some hands-on experience."

"That was Dad's doing. He would drag me away from my room under the guise of needing help. He just wanted to spend some time with me. I didn't appreciate it then, but I do now. I wasn't a total brat. There was a part of me that always knew how hard he worked. He never wanted me to end up in the factories for a paycheck. It was honest and important work, and I wished I had told him that more often. I suppose everyone has similar regrets when they think about their parents."

"That's part of growing up. You could have related to my father; he was an accountant. You would have had numbers in common."

She was enjoying their conversation and wanted to know more about his life. "Did your mother work outside the home?"

"Not when we were little. My brother was a full-time job for her due to his heart condition. Later, when we were in high school, she became a counselor for families going through medical crises like what we went through."

Smiling, Laurel replied, "Lemons into lemonade."

"Precisely. Her only failing was her sarcastic wit. Sometimes she could offend people with it, but once they knew her, people realized she had a heart of gold."

"I've met a few people like that, and I loved them. My mother was just the opposite. She carefully considered every word that came out of her mouth. She said it had something to do with trying to put toothpaste back in the tube."

David nearly choked with laughter. "You could have scraped the toothpaste off my mother."

He finished his coffee. "It's getting late. I had better go. May I call you again?"

She walked him to the front door. "I'd like that very much."

He pulled her toward him and kissed her. She lingered in an embrace, feeling the warmth from his body and the scent of his cologne. He turned to head for his car as she closed the door. She leaned her back against it and smiled with a contentment which had for so long eluded her.

Chapter Nine

"Tell me everything," Janet said when she called to find out about Laurel's date.

"It was nice."

"Just nice? Surely you have more to report than that. Where did he take you?"

"Autumn Hill Inn."

"Was it awkward?" Janet asked after a long pause. "I know it was one of your favorite places. We even went there a few times on a couples date with our husbands."

"It was at first. Mr. Zander came over to our table, but he seemed sensitive enough to realize he shouldn't say much. He did, however, call me Mrs. Tanner."

"What did Dr. Bradford say?"

"He said he already knew who I was because he had his accounts at the bank."

Janet had often waited on him. "That's right, he does. It's better that you have it out in the open. It's not like you robbed the bank."

"He's had relationship problems too. I'm certain it helped each of us to talk about them. I mentioned Missy, but he wouldn't even acknowledge she was his patient. He said he couldn't speak about any patient without express permission. I respect him for that because I never discussed a customer's business. Ethical issues are important to both of us."

"Next time I take Missy in, I'll tell him he can speak to you if you have questions. It's too critical an issue to worry about confidentiality. You may learn something that can benefit the foundation and help children like Missy."

"I just assumed you would take her to an oncologist at the children's hospital," Laurel said.

"Dr. Bradford is still her pediatrician, and I trust him to supervise her treatments. When we chose him to be the kids' doctor, we carefully researched his background. After all, the children are our life. When something catastrophic happens, you lose some of that control. He personally chose Dr. Kaminsky for Missy's treatments. We trust his judgment implicitly."

"I met Dr. Kaminsky at the conference. I had a feeling that was the doctor who was treating her. I mentioned I had a friend whose child was ill, and when I said her name, he seemed to react to it but naturally did not tell me that she was his patient. I can find out more about him if you wish."

"It's not necessary. We checked several sources after Dr. Bradford suggested him; that coupled with his recommendation was enough to convince us she's in good hands. He's an extremely serious man, but he manages to turn that off when he's with Missy."

"It takes teamwork, and it seems as though you have it under control."

"No one has anything under control when their child is sick. We are doing the best we can under the circumstances."

Laurel replied, "It sounds like it, and I will keep on top of anything that might help Missy."

They ended their conversation, but it left Laurel a

little restless. She filled a bucket of feed to take to the cemetery to feed the swans. It was midafternoon before she arrived. The sunshine-filled day had dozens of people jogging and walking their pets. She even spotted a couple of children fishing. She worried for a moment that the swans may go after the hook if they thought there was food involved. She quickly realized they were too clever for that mistake.

She walked to the water's edge and made a chirping sound to attract the birds. Her attempt was pathetic, but they recognized the bucket in her hand and came over for their treats. She tossed handfuls out to them, and their heads bobbed up and down in the water.

A young girl appeared by her side and asked, "Can I give them some?"

Laurel smiled. "Help yourself."

The child grabbed a handful, which was minimal, and tossed it onto the water. Most of it landed on the water's edge but Laurel knew it would be picked up eventually.

"Oh, I missed," she said, looking disappointed.

She was adorable in a little pink dress with a matching straw hat. Laurel surmised they had attended church and stopped by the cemetery to either take in nature or visit a family member's grave.

Laurel heard a woman call, "Emma, don't fall in the water."

"I'm being careful, Mommy," she said with a hint of disgust at being stopped from having a little innocent fun. It was then a gust of wind came out of nowhere, and the little girl's hat flew off her head and onto the ground. As she scrambled to retrieve it, Laurel saw what she was trying to conceal; the little girl had no hair. Her mother ran to her, afraid the child would cry, but she did not.

"Let's get home, honey. Thank the nice lady for letting you feed the swans."

"Thank you," she said politely.

"It was my, and the swans', pleasure." Laurel felt like she had a rock in the pit of her stomach as she watched the little girl skip away. She wondered if that would soon be Missy and nearly cried at the thought. She dumped the rest of the bucket of feed into the pond and started walking up a hill toward her parents' grave. As she approached a V on the driveway, she met up with Maggie.

"I saw you down by the pond with a little girl."

Laurel sighed. "The poor little thing must be going through chemotherapy. She was bald."

"I thought maybe that was your friend's little girl."

Laurel shook her head. "No, but it will be. How do families get through something like that?"

"One day at a time and faith in a higher power."

Laurel needed clarity. "Have you ever gone through something like that?"

She nodded. "We all have in one form or another. Sometimes it's life or death. Sometimes it only seems that way."

Laurel thought about her father's illness, her mother's death, and Chaz's betrayal. "You're right. I've been there."

Maggie said, "I thought as much. The first time I saw you, there was a lost sadness in you."

"How did you know that?"

"Most of what people convey to you is nonverbal. Your tone and attitude spoke volumes. In fact, it seems to be saying something different now."

There was a glint in the old woman's eye that made Laurel smile. "And what would that be?"

"You dated that doctor."

Laurel was astounded by her intuition. "How did you know that?"

"I'm old, not blind. I saw him jogging through here earlier this morning, and there was a pep to him I hadn't seen before."

"This morning? Do you live here?"

She shrugged. "So to speak."

Concerned the old woman spent too much time alone, she asked, "Do you have any family to spend your time with?"

"Certainly, I have two children. They are grown now and on their own, but I see them or at least one of them daily."

Laurel wanted to ask about a husband but did not. Maggie may have been divorced under acrimonious circumstances, and she did not want to bring up any unhappy memories. She had been through too much herself to be intrusive, though she thought the spunky old woman was hardly the type to be offended by much of anything.

She felt better knowing Maggie had family nearby. "As long as you're not alone."

"I'm never alone and never lonely. Now, give me the details on the hunky doctor."

Laurel blushed. "It was nice. We had a lovely dinner at Autumn Hill Inn and talked."

Raising her eyebrows, Maggie asked, "Just talk?"

"Yes," Laurel said, pretending to not understand her meaning.

"Are you going to see him again?"

Nodding Laurel replied, "I think so."

"Just *think*?"

"I had a horrific experience with my ex-husband. I don't know how much I want to put myself out there."

"Ah, we've all had them. I'm sure even the good doctor has had a few."

"He has. I guess we both need to tread lightly."

"Nothing wrong with that, as long as you are treading."

"I've been through one of the most trying times in my life this past year."

"And you've been white-knuckling it alone, right?"

"Was it that obvious?"

"To an old woman it is so don't be afraid to move forward. Take all the time you need but do it. People like you and Dr. Hunky have too much to offer this world to barricade yourselves from it."

Laurel smiled. "Thank you, it's nice to speak with someone who has a detached perspective. My friends are exceedingly kind but too one-sided on my behalf."

The old woman laughed and asked, "Would you want it the other way around?"

Laughing too, Laurel replied, "I suppose not."

"It's been nice talking with you, dear. I'm glad to see you're doing well."

Laurel waved to her as Maggie continued her walk. She then made her way to her parents' grave and said a quick prayer for them before heading back to her car parked near the pond. She had intended on doing some yard work, but as she looked up into the sky, dark clouds had formed and a storm was imminent. She barely made it home before the sky opened with a torrential downpour.

It was as dark as night as she turned on a lamp. It began to flicker when she heard the thunder and saw flashes of lightening. She remembered a college roommate who was terrified by thunderstorms, but Laurel loved them. When she was a child, she recalled the first time she experienced the loud claps of thunder which shook the house. She went crying to her mother in fear. Her mother gently rocked her telling her it was nothing to be afraid of. In fact, it turned out to be fun.

When the power went out, her parents lit scented candles and read her stories. It completely changed her perspective, and it has remained with her all through the years. In fact, Laurel turned off the lights, lit some candles, and reached for a book. She felt her parents' love in every familiar thing in the house, and it gave her a sense of peace.

She did not welcome it, but she also thought about Chaz. Their first date ended with them being caught in Central Park during a thunderstorm. They had rented bicycles and were meandering the paths when out of nowhere a storm began. They looked like two drowned rats by the time they could return the bikes. She went back to his apartment to dry off and had a memorable romantic evening. She had even considered it a good omen because of her childhood memories. So much for good omens—she thought to herself.

She set her book aside and went to make a cup of tea only to discover the power had gone out. She was still able to light the gas stove and put the tea kettle on. She took the steaming hot cup back to her chair, picked up her book, and then heard a deafening sound. Lightning had struck a tree near the road, and it fell across her driveway. Fortunately, it was not near her house, or it would have caused substantial damage. She would not be able to drive out her driveway because there was a ditch on either side too steep to go through. It did not concern her too much because she had nowhere she had to go, and the highway department would undoubtedly clear it because some of it had fallen into the street.

She returned to her chair and book, and within a half hour, she heard a chainsaw revving near the road. She looked out the window expecting to see the flashing lights of the highway department, but all she saw was a car parked near the road and a man cutting up the tree in the driving rain. She put on her raincoat, flipped up the hood, and headed down her driveway. She was more than a little surprised to see David buzzing up just enough pieces of the tree to clear her driveway.

She called loudly to him to be heard over the chainsaw. "What in heaven's name are you doing out in this storm?"

He shut it off to reply. "When the power went out, I thought I'd check on you, but when I got here, I saw the tree. I drove back home to grab my chainsaw."

She shouted over the pounding rain. "David, this is insane. There could be another lightning strike. It could wait until the storm cleared."

Rain was dripping down his face when he said, "I didn't want you to feel trapped here. I don't leave anything to chance."

"I can understand. You're a doctor with real emergencies. I don't have to worry about that."

"I'll explain after you help me push a few of these

pieces of tree off to the side."

They rolled just enough of the tree to clear the end of her driveway so he could pull his car up to the house. "I can't come in and drip water everywhere," he said.

"But you can't go home like that?"

"It's not that far. I can drive home in a few minutes."

"Your car seats will get soaked. Just come in and…"

He interrupted her. "And what? Put on your bathrobe. I doubt you have a closet filled with men's clothing."

"You can wrap yourself in a blanket, and I'll hang your clothes near the fireplace. They'll dry out, and if the power comes back on, I'll throw them in the dryer."

He had a smirk on his face when he asked, "Is this a trick to get me out of my clothes?"

She giggled. "Did it work?"

Shivering he replied, "Yep. Get me a blanket."

"I have just the thing for you." She went into her linen closet and brought out a gift her mother had bought her, a blanket that zipped around a person for snuggling on the sofa on a chilly night. He took it into her bathroom and returned to model it for her. She laughed hysterically at the sight. "It's you," she said.

He spun in a circle to show it off and flopped down on the sofa next to her. "I hung my wet clothes in the shower."

"This is the first major storm we've had since I've been back home. Does the power usually stay off for very long?"

He shook his head. "Not generally. There is a new substation for the electrical grid nearby, so we're usually one of the first to get power restored."

She went into the kitchen to make another cup of tea for herself and David. He gratefully took a sip of the hot tea, warming his hands on the cup.

"What did you mean you'd explain about the need to clear my driveway?"

He was still shivering a bit when he took another sip of the blessedly hot tea. "I told you about my little brother's heart defect."

She nodded.

"You know how brutal the winters can be here. We once had a major snowstorm which blocked our driveway. My brother had a medical emergency, and my parents couldn't get him to the hospital. They called an ambulance, but the roads were in poor condition, which slowed everything down and then they had to trudge through the snow to the house. After that, my parents never left anything to chance again. It has stuck with me. Rationally, I know it didn't make much of a difference if you couldn't get down the driveway, but you never know what's around the corner."

She was touched by his thoughtfulness. "It was kind of you to be so concerned.

He looked at her with an almost puzzled expression. "Do you have any idea how it feels to care about someone again after you have been hurt?"

"I know exactly how that feels."

He leaned into her, tenderly caressing her cheek with his fingers. Looking into her beautiful green eyes, he gave her a kiss which she readily returned. As it turned out, he had plenty of time for his clothes to dry because he never made it back home that night.

Chapter Ten

When Laurel opened eyes the following morning, David was lying on his side beside her with his head propped on one arm. She smiled. "Good morning."

He reached over and gently whisked a lock of hair from her eyes. "Any regrets?"

"None."

"At the risk of sounding ungentlemanly, I've only got an hour to go home, shower, shave, and change before my first appointment."

"Your clothes should be dry by now. "

"I guess I'll find out." He slipped into the bathroom to dress. When he returned, he said, "Believe it or not the jeans are still a little damp."

"The power is on; I could toss them in the dryer for a few minutes."

"It doesn't matter one way or another; I have to change anyway."

"Let me at least fix you a cup of coffee."

He sat on the edge of the bed next to her. "I don't want you to get out of bed. I like the image of you lying here. I'll let myself out and lock up. I'll give you a call later."

He lingered in the doorway for a few minutes with a playful smirk on his face. "You weren't just using me as your play toy?"

She laughed. "You'll never know."

After she heard the front door shut, she snuggled beneath the sheets. She had not felt this relaxed since the whole mess with Chaz began. There was something about David's genuine empathy that put her at ease. She was confident he felt the same way about her. Where they were headed she did not know, and in that moment it did not even matter. She was tired of always planning out every minute detail of her life. She had never been a spontaneous person, and she liked how it felt.

****

David made it to his office with five minutes to spare before his first patient arrived. His nurse eyed him suspiciously as he whistled between patients. As he sat in his office reviewing a patient chart, his nurse stood in the doorway watching him. "Okay, who are you and what have you done with the real Dr. Bradford?"

He leaned back in his desk chair and smiled. "What are you talking about?"

With a snort, she rolled her eyes. "You got lucky, didn't you?"

"Could you be cruder?" he asked, pretending to be offended.

His nurse had been with him since he began his practice. They were more than employer/employee; they were close friends. She had been a kind and sympathetic ear when he needed one. They could say anything to each other in playful banter. "I could, but I'll let it go at that."

He handed her a chart. "I don't kiss and tell."

"Finally, one of your blind dates paid off."

He was casual in his response. "I found this one on my own, thank you."

His intercom buzzed and his receptionist said, "Dr.

Bradford, Mrs. Miller is on line one. It sounds urgent."

He pressed the button and asked in a concerned tone, "What's wrong, Janet?"

"It's Missy. She's running a high fever."

"Bring her in immediately."

A short while later, Janet came into his office carrying the child who was as limp as a ragdoll. David took Missy from her arms and into an exam room with both his nurse and Janet close behind. The child was too lethargic to even speak.

He took her temperature and examined the result. "How long has she been like this?"

"She woke up with the fever. I checked on her during the night, and she seemed fine."

"We can't be too careful. I want her admitted to the hospital at once. Even had I not known she has leukemia, her temperature alone would warrant admission."

He then looked over at his nurse. "Tracy, call an ambulance."

Janet was horrified. "Wouldn't it be faster if I just drove her?"

He put his hand on her shoulder to reason with her. "It may be faster, but not safer. You can't keep an eye on Missy and drive at the same time."

"Can I at least ride in the ambulance?"

"I'm certain they won't mind. I'll call ahead to Dr. Kaminski."

****

Laurel was at home working on projection numbers for the next fundraiser when David called. She saw his name on the caller ID and answered before it went to voice mail. "I didn't think I'd hear from you so soon."

His tone was somber. "I wish you weren't."

She clicked off her computer screen to give him her full attention. She knew he wasn't about to tell her anything good. "What's wrong?"

"Janet asked me to call you. She brought Missy in with a high fever, and I sent them by ambulance to the children's hospital."

Her instincts were correct. "Oh, no, is it bad?"

"I'm not an alarmist. Kids get fevers all the time, but when you're treating a child with leukemia, it's necessary to err on the side of caution."

"What can I do?"

"Probably nothing more than moral support."

"I'll head right over there. Her husband is out of town on business, and I know her in-laws would be with her son. She might need someone."

"It would be good for her to see a friendly face. Call me when you get a chance."

She found Janet sitting in a waiting room while some tests were being performed on Missy. When she saw Laurel approach, she stood up and hugged her.

"Have they told you anything yet?" Laurel asked.

Janet shook her head. "No, but they told me not to panic. This is a common symptom to expect. I'm certain they are going to tell us she must start the chemo soon. The blood work will be the indicator."

She started to sob. "How do I tell her she is going to lose her hair and be horribly sick?"

Laurel couldn't control her own tears. "I wish I had an answer for you. I'll bring you all the literature we have at the foundation for support groups. She will be with other children going through the same thing, so she won't seem different."

"Mike," Janet shouted as she saw her husband come through the door and ran into his arms.

"I got here as soon as I could. Have you heard anything yet?"

"I'll leave you two alone. Call me if you need anything, and I mean anything," Laurel said, giving each of them a hug.

She was in the city anyway, so she went to her office. She called her assistant in and asked for any brochures they had on the support groups. Within minutes, she returned with several pamphlets. The one she thought Janet could use first was explaining to siblings about their brother or sister's illness. It dealt with a complex of emotions from fear, jealousy, and survivors' guilt. When a family member is sick the whole family suffers.

She called David from her car on the drive home. "They're running tests, but it looks like she will end up starting chemo."

"I'll call Dr. Kaminsky tomorrow and follow up. How is Janet doing?"

"Her husband made it to the hospital. I think they have been expecting this."

"How far are you from the diner in town?"

"Maybe fifteen minutes; why?"

"I'll buy you dinner, and we can talk."

****

David was already seated by the time she arrived. As she came through the door, he lifted his hand to wave her over. He stood when she approached the booth, leaned over, and gave her a quick kiss. It was a simple but intimate gesture.

"It has seemed like a long day."

"I'll bet. I like my days to consist of giving out lollipops after an inoculation or doing wellness check-ups. Missy was my only serious case."

"Janet and Mike look so exhausted."

"It will get worse before it gets better. If there is any bright light, it's the type of leukemia Missy developed. Seventy-five percent of all children who have leukemia have that variety, and it has a ninety percent cure rate."

"I'd take those odds," Laurel replied.

"You wouldn't if you were Janet. For any parent, even a ten percent mortality rate is too high."

She could feel his compassion for his patients when he said that, which prompted her to ask, "Why did you choose to become a doctor and the field of pediatrics?"

The waitress came by with glasses of water and to take their order. She looked at Laurel and asked, "Two specials?"

At Laurel's nod, the waitress left them to continue their conversation.

"I don't know that I would say I chose medicine; it chose me. It felt right. Maybe it had something to do with my little brother. I can remember feeling so helpless when he would be in the hospital and having endless surgeries. My parents were great, but just as you have seen with the Millers, the stress is horrendous. I thought if I could ever alleviate some of that for other people, I wanted to do it."

"So, it was a calling, not a selection."

He took a sip of water before replying. "I guess you could call it that; I never really put it into words."

She smiled. "Whatever name you want to give it,

it's commendable."

He shrugged. "It took over too much of my life. I told you that's why my engagement ended. I'm trying to balance a personal life with a professional, but sometimes they overlap."

She uttered, "And sometimes we're forced to change course."

He reached over to take her hand, asking, "How are you with that, really?"

"Six months ago, if you'd asked me that question and I had been offered this job—I would have said I was settling. It's not that I thought it's beneath me. This is important work in its own right. I came from a fast-paced, intense financial world where profit and results were mandatory. Coming to Bridgefield to assume the position of bank president and overseeing acquisitions of nearby banks was a career downgrade. Surprisingly, that didn't matter to me. My small-town roots surfaced, but I still needed the engagement that the financial world I came from challenged in me. I remember my husband telling me we could be *big fish in a small pond*. I never needed the validation of others he did, but I would be lying if I did not admit I liked the respect that came with my job."

"There is nothing wrong with that, and from what I've discerned, you had earned that respect. Your fall from grace was not of your making."

"Does that matter? It still stings that it's a blemish on my character."

He sounded like a preacher when he said, "It does matter when you look into the mirror. The person you must do right by is yourself. You must matter to you and no one else first, or you cannot move forward."

His words had a familiar ring to them, and she remembered her elderly friend Maggie had made a remarkably similar statement about herself. Laurel now realized she was subtly trying to tell her the same thing David had said.

"I'm beginning to believe I was meant to change direction."

"What makes you say that?"

"My parents sacrificed so much for my education. I realize that no small part of my ambition was for their benefit. I'll admit, money was a motivator, but not just for myself. I don't need, in fact I don't want, a lavish lifestyle, but I did need to repay my parents. It all seemed to be lumped together. My father died before I could be of any real help to him. I was able to help my mother. I wanted to spoil her with all the material things she couldn't give me, but things she did give me were more valuable."

"Did she know that? I know I should have made that clearer to my parents."

Laurel smiled. "Yes; that was the one thing I did right. I told her that, and she said it was all part of being a parent. One day when I had children I would understand."

"So, what has changed?"

"That should be obvious," she began, almost sarcastically. "They're gone."

"And you don't need more?"

"I don't. I never wanted them to need anything, and I did what I could, but my ex-husband had an insatiable appetite for success. When my mother died, so did that need inside me. I kept on the same path because it was so important to Chaz. I had no idea he would risk people's financial security, not to mention ours."

"You saw where that went," David said.

"I haven't fully come to terms with that, and I'm trying not to let it weigh on me. I am in a better place now, but I still have baggage from my past."

The waitress came and momentarily interrupted their conversation by placing their meals in front of them. David thanked her before she disappeared into the kitchen. He then reached for Laurel's hand. "We all have baggage. It's not necessarily a bad thing."

She looked surprised. "You told me your fiancée broke your heart."

He nodded. "But did she? Maybe I broke my own heart, and it was easier to blame her."

"Are you purposely talking in riddles?"

He took the time to take a bite of his food and swallow before answering. "Ultimately, it was my actions that caused the break-up. Granted, she handled it badly. She had plenty of time to call it off before it became so close to the wedding. Maybe if she had sat me down and explained her feelings, I would have tried to change."

"You did change."

He shrugged. "Like yours, it was a forced change. Trust me it didn't come easily. I still wonder what I might have done differently."

"Do you still love her?" she asked, almost afraid of his answer.

He took a deep breath before replying. "No, and that scares me more than telling you I do. I've asked myself a million times if she hadn't called off the wedding, would we be happy. I'm not convinced we were suited for each other."

She was a little envious he had gotten to that point of his healing, while she was still struggling with it. "That knowledge must give you some relief."

The turn in the conversation was making him uneasy. "Let me ask you the same question; do you still love your ex-husband?"

She intently looked into his eyes. "The truth?"

He nodded. "Of course."

"I don't know."

He seemed offended by her response. "Wow."

It was her turn to reach over and take his hand saying, "Please don't think it has anything to do with you. You are three years ahead of me in the healing process and have had plenty of time to think it over. I'm still trying to sort out the man I knew, loved, and married, from the one who betrayed me and the principles I thought we were living by."

She could see the anger on his face. His lips pursed, and his cheeks reddened. His voice became curt. "I think we should change the subject and revisit this another time."

They finished their dinner in awkward silence.

When he had paid the check and was walking her to her car, she waited for him to give her a kiss. It never happened, he simply said, "I'll call you tomorrow. Hopefully, we will know more about Missy by then."

Laurel got into her car and sat silently behind the wheel trying to think how she could have turned a pleasant dinner into an uncomfortable ending. She genuinely cared about David, and she thought he fully understood her dilemma. She was understanding of his and the journey he had taken to be happy. Why couldn't he give her that same courtesy?

She did not want to repeat her past mistake of giving too much of herself to her own detriment. She had made substantial strides and wanted David to understand and not shut down on her the first time they had an honest discussion.

Chapter Eleven

David had a restless night. When it was barely light, he decided to burn off his frustration by running at Pioneer Cemetery. His was the only car parked near the road, which was common at that hour. He did not just jog; he ran like a madman, tiring himself out on the hilly driveways. As he headed up one of the hills, he thought something looked different, more spacious. When he got to the summit, he realized why; an enormous oak tree had fallen. He surmised it was likely the victim of the same storm which took the tree down at Laurel's house. As he approached the tree, he saw the damage it had caused, and all the branches had been removed by the maintenance crew. Only the main trunk remained with someone sitting on it. It was the stranger who had helped him three years prior when he had his meltdown.

He walked up to her. "What a shame."

She nodded in agreement. "I guess we all have to go sometime." Then she added, "You're awfully early. Usually, you are arriving just as I am leaving."

He was out of breath from his run. "May I sit?"

"Oh certainly," she replied patting the bark of the tree. "I was just waiting for my friend who walks with me. She is characteristically late."

Looking around he asked, "Why did they leave the trunk here?"

"One of the groundskeepers said it was being milled. They thought they may be able to use the lumber for some local projects."

"I like that idea. It makes sense."

The woman offered him a direct look. "What demon is chasing you today?"

He was still feeling uneasy about his conversation with Laurel and wasn't certain he wanted to explain. He answered her question with a question. "What makes you think one is?"

"Instinct and the sweat rolling down your face. I've never seen you run like that before. Either you're in great physical shape or working out a problem."

She spoke with the same kindness he remembered from before. He asked, "Am I that transparent?"

"Not really, I just recognize the signs. You aren't the only person who comes here to work out their frustrations. Last week I saw a young woman riding her bicycle in much the same manner you were running. A short while later, a man drove in, found her, and they ended up in a touching embrace."

He snorted a short laugh. "I'm not unique, then?"

"You're just human."

"I've never had the opportunity to thank you after you helped me. I needed to let it out."

"It's sometimes easier and safer to vent to a total stranger. I'm glad I was able to help, but something tells me you need to do the same thing again."

"Do you mind?"

With a wave of her hand, she replied, "Have at it."

He gave her the condensed version of Laurel's past and their recent conversation. She listened intently. "It sounds like you're painting her with your brush."

"I'm not sure I know what you're getting at."

"She's been through a lot this past year, and she still needs to figure out some things. Don't forget she was married for several years; you were only engaged."

He was a little perturbed that she didn't readily see his point. "I don't see why that is so different. The principle is the same."

"Only in the most minor sense. Marriage is difficult, even when it works. There are compromises and sacrifices, shared joys, and dreams. I'm not saying you were not entitled to your hurt feelings and anger, but there is a distinct difference between what you both have gone through."

"Are you married?"

Her face took on a sweet, serene look. "I've been married forever, and I can't think of another man I'd trade him for."

"See; that's what I want. I want to be sitting here at your age being able to say the same thing about my wife."

"And you could be if you don't let your ego get in the way."

He thought about his own parents. "I guess it's possible. My folks were married for forty years."

"Then you have an excellent example. Were they happy?"

He started laughing. "If they weren't, my mother would never have let my father state otherwise. She was a real spitfire."

The woman leaned backed and roared out a laugh. "And I bet your father adored her for it."

Still smiling he said, "Usually, but they could get into some pretty heated arguments."

"All couples do. If they don't fight, they probably aren't in love. If you don't care about someone, you don't have the need to provoke them. The response is everything, but the reason is usually inconsequential."

"So, you have arguments with your husband?"

There was a smirk on her face when she answered. "We're on the same plane now but we did when we were younger. Everything seems so much more intense when you're young."

"What do you suggest I do?" he asked hoping she had something tangible he could grasp onto.

"What kind of woman is she? Is she like your mother and a spitfire, as you put it?"

He laughed again, and it felt good. "The exact opposite. She's more like you; thoughtful, soft-spoken, and considerate."

"If that's your opinion of her, you need to give her a break. Don't ever make her think she can't tell you what she is really thinking because it will haunt your relationship. If you can talk through your differences, they won't seem as important."

"Do you have children?"

"I do, and that is the same advice I would give them."

He stood to leave. "Thank you. I really mean it."

He jogged back in the direction of his car leaving her to wait for her friend to arrive. Before he left, he saw her from a distance walking with another woman. Her tardy friend must have finally arrived.

****

After showering and changing, David went to work, but his mind wasn't with his body.

His nurse asked, "What's wrong with you? This is

121

the third time you've grabbed the wrong chart."

He gave her a weak smile. "I didn't grab the wrong chart. You gave me the wrong patient."

"Yesterday your feet barely touched the ground. What has changed since then?"

"Hopefully, nothing," he said. "Was that our last patient?"

"Yes, get out of here; you're driving me crazy," she said, swatting him with a file.

"Thanks, Tracy."

On his way home, he dropped by the grocery store before heading to Laurel's house. He rang her doorbell, and when she answered, he handed her his purchase.

"A jar of olives?"

He had hoped to break the ice with the gift. "They didn't have any olive branches; this was as close as I could get."

Gesturing with her head, she pointed for him to enter.

"I acted like a jerk."

She let him sit on the sofa and then sat opposite him in a chair before replying. "You weren't a jerk. I understand how you felt because I would have felt the same way if you had told me you still loved your fiancée. If I have any argument with you at all, it was you didn't give me a chance to clarify."

He bowed his head a bit. "I'm not certain I even have the right to expect you to do that. We're still getting to know each other. We've only been on one date."

"And slept together," she reminded him. "That meant something. I can assure you I have never been that impulsive. I felt an inexplicable closeness to you."

"And I you. Something has been missing in each of us, and we found it that night. I think that's what worried me—that it might end before it had a chance to begin."

The intensity in her voice was palpable. "I don't think that will be the case. I'm still in a bit of a fog, and you'll have to bear with me. I'm trying to sort out who Chaz really was; it's a reflection on me as well as him. I have always been so serious and one-dimensional, saying and doing the right things. He was the fun side of me, because he wanted it all and embraced everything."

"Including taking other people's money and ruining their lives and your career?"

"That's my disconnect. I should hate him, but I also can never forget his tenderness toward my mother and the love I know he had for me. What am I supposed to do about that?"

"Couldn't he have been both? Life isn't always so black and white. We make mistakes, learn from them, and hopefully do the right thing. He didn't get that last part right."

"That's probably the kindest explanation you could have given me, and likely the most accurate. Now that I have had some time to reflect, I realize he was a weak man, not a bad one. He was as driven as I was for different reasons. His family life was less than loving. I believe he always had a need for success and wealth so he could say to his parents, 'See how important I am.' When he started buying expensive things, it was that side of him which was emerging. I should have seen that. I, on the other hand, wanted success for security and knowing my parents' belief in me was justified. It gave me such pleasure doing things for my mother."

He listened to her as she spoke from her heart. "Do you realize that same satisfaction you got from helping your mother has transferred to helping others with your work at the foundation? If Chaz were still here, where would you be?"

"Where I was before he left; running the bank and its acquisitions, crunching numbers, and acting as his support person."

"What about having your own family? Weren't children even considered?"

"Oh yes, we talked about a family, but he always had a reason for postponing it. He probably wanted to be the only child in our marriage."

"Regardless of what he did, your marriage would not have survived. It's necessary for you to realize that. He would have kept the real you from coming out because he needed everything to stay the same. It would have eventually devoured you."

"And now you know what I am struggling with. Do you think it is too simplistic to call all this a *blessing in disguise*?"

He leaned back into the sofa and sighed. "I don't know if that's the simplistic answer, but it certainly is true. Some of the best things which happen to people have been forced on them. You had no reason to look beyond him and the life you made, especially without your mother to be an allied observer. He may have cared for her, but trust me, no mother would side against their child. You would know."

Laurel laughed lightly. "Especially mine. She was careful to never impose her opinions, but she had a way of giving them. However, if she had any misgivings, she didn't express them, maybe because the change in Chaz happened after her death."

He stood and was walking toward her fireplace when he said, "My mother would impose them and not be apologetic about it. If she had been alive when my fiancée left me, she would have given her a black eye." He then looked at the photo on her mantel of her parents' wedding day and picked it up. "Your mother looks vaguely familiar."

Laurel came over to him smiling and pointed to herself. He looked at the photo and then at Laurel. "You could have been sisters at the same age."

"I'll take that as a compliment."

"Oh, it genuinely is. Your mother was a very beautiful woman."

She took the photo from his hand and placed it back on the mantel. "Inside and out."

He reached for her, pulling her into his arms. "I want you to know, I'm not Chaz. I want you to be the person you need to be. No one should stand in your way. It's all very confusing for you right now, and you're entitled to have any feelings you have toward him. Make sure you aren't looking through clouded glasses. I mean that in both extremes. Don't let yourself become nostalgic and question his culpability, but also don't hate him. In fact, that might be worse because then you'd hate yourself by having been taken advantage of."

She leaned into his chest and uttered, "Where do we go from here?"

He whispered as he nuzzled her ear, "Any place you want."

****

Before Laurel could respond to that intriguing comment her phone rang. "Janet. How is Missy?" she asked, pointing to the phone for David to pay attention.

Weariness was obvious in Janet's tone when she said, "Missy's been admitted indefinitely. They are going to start chemo."

"I'm sorry. David is here. Would you like to speak with him?"

He took the phone from Laurel and placed it on speaker so they both could hear the conversation. "Janet, you may not want to hear this, but the sooner treatments start, the better."

"I know that logically, but my heart says otherwise."

"I'll call Dr. Kaminsky first thing in the morning. Missy is in good hands, and he won't steer you wrong. If he says it's time to start treatment, then I would not question him."

Laurel heard Janet sobbing. "I've never spent a single night away from her."

"Children are resilient and accepting. Every nurse, doctor, and orderly knows how to comfort the children. Missy will bond with the other kids, and they will be one of her greatest support resources." His voice was so calm and reassuring it melted Laurel's heart. It was another dimension that made him special.

Janet's weeping came over the phone. "But they're not her mother."

"I know your heart is breaking right now," he said. "It's necessary for you to remember you have another child who needs you. He's too young to fully grasp what's going on, and he needs his mom to reassure him everything is going to be all right. You've got to remain strong for both your children."

He handed the phone back to Laurel, who asked Janet if she wanted her to come over for support.

"Thanks for offering but there's nothing you can do."

Laurel herself was in tears. "Okay. I'll call you in the morning."

Laurel was in no way trying to criticize David, but she asked, "Do you think it was wise to suggest she needs to be with her son? She is already feeling guilty about leaving Missy."

"Do you suppose you could turn those olives into a martini?"

"Of course." She went into the kitchen to prepare a pitcher of them. She needed a drink, too. When she returned, he answered her question.

"What I said to Janet was intentional. You may agree or disagree with my methods, but I've been down this road before. She loves her daughter above herself. She wants to be there for her and take the pain away."

"What's so wrong about that?"

"When I was a resident, doing a rotation in the emergency room, a mother brought her child in who was bleeding from some broken glass. It wasn't severe, but it did require sutures. The first thing the attending doctor did was make the mother leave while we treated the child. I initially thought she should remain to calm the child because he was crying hysterically. The doctor explained to me that the child would feed off the mother's anxiety and it would be much harder to attend to him. He was right. Once the mother left, he listened to what we had to say and was remarkably brave for a young child. Had his mother been there he would have clung to her, and they both would have been a mess. The situation with Janet and Missy is not dissimilar. Janet is going to have to let go and let the staff at the hospital do what they must do. Certainly, there will be instances where Missy will be afraid, but she will be forced to listen to the people who know best. Unlike a child who is getting a few sutures, she is in for a much longer and involved procedure. It's imperative the doctors and nurses are not met with resistance. She is not being cut out of any treatments or from seeing her daughter, but there are times it would be best for all involved she not be hovering over them."

"I understand the wisdom of your logic, but I wouldn't want to be the person to say that to Janet. Right now, it's Missy's heart beating in her chest."

David was silent as he made himself another martini. Laurel studied his expression. He seemed to be in another place, and she wished she could read his mind. When he turned and saw her looking at him, he smiled. It was that simple smile that filled her with a complete sense of well-being and love.

Chapter Twelve

David finished his drink and bent over to kiss Laurel goodbye. "I don't want you to leave before we have a chance to talk," she said reaching for his hand.

"I needed to apologize, and I thought you might need some space."

"I appreciate your thoughtfulness," she said pulling him down beside her. "Maybe I'm being overly cautious in moving ahead in our relationship. I don't want to rush into something, but I also don't want to push you away. I'm trying to stand on my own two feet and not lean on someone else."

"Sometimes we need to lean on someone else."

She gently placed a finger on his lips to silence him while she explained. "I've never been a needy person, but I've never been tested. I had the blessing of wonderful parents, an Ivy League education, a great career, and what I thought was a loving marriage. It was my marriage which has shaken my confidence. I never want to be that vulnerable and wrong again."

David shook his head. "I'm not Chaz."

She didn't want to offend him and quickly clarified. "I know you're not. My ex-husband, for all his boasting, was extremely insecure. That his Achilles heel and led to his downfall. He wanted too much, too fast. The sad part about it—he was good at what he did. I mourned more for what he could have been, than what he lost. You're the complete antithesis; modest and confident. I've seen that in the way you have handled Missy's illness and the family's anxiety. You don't have the need to stand on a pedestal and be worshipped."

"I didn't know that was an option," he said with a laugh, lightening the mood.

She laughed, too. "We have traveled a similar road from our family to our respective heartbreak, and it has brought us here. I needed to find my voice and believe in a kinder, gentler side of people."

His eyebrows furrowed with confusion when he said, "You have, and I suspect that was the person you always were. I also suspect Chaz took advantage of that. Is that what you're worried about?"

"Is it so different from your experience with your fiancée?"

"In principle, I suppose it's not. She had many of the insecurities you said Chaz possessed, and I guess she thought the wife of a doctor would fill the void. She didn't realize the sacrifices that would go with it. I was often on call or taking calls from patients. Our wedding rehearsal dinner was apparently the last straw for her. I had to leave for an emergency, and she suddenly realized that would be our life together and she wanted no part of it. She didn't even have the decency to say that to my face. I received a cold impersonal letter, hand delivered by one of her friends detailing my failings. I must have reread that letter a hundred times."

Laurel could feel his anguish and touched his cheek with a gentle stroke. "Do you still have the letter?"

Shaking his head, he said, "I burned it after making

love to you. It no longer had a place in my life."
****

Laurel and David talked every day and dined together often but tone-downed their physical attraction. They wanted things to be right and it was worth waiting to be sure. It was just as well because Laurel had her hands full organizing the upcoming fundraiser. This had been the foundation's major annual event, and everything had to be perfect. In the past she had been a guest, not an organizer. When she had previously volunteered, it was for their small, informal events such as picnics and auctions. This was a formal black-tie event which catered to wealthy members of the business community and corporate sponsors.

The foundation had a standing arrangement with the convention center in the city to rent the ballroom. She had been grateful that her assistant had a detailed list of how the fundraiser was organized. She was pleased with the overall arrangements, but she needed to put her own stamp on it to be unique. She decided to emphasize the importance of community. She wanted the patrons to feel the impact their contributions were making. Most of the children being served at the Children's Hospital were from the region. She wanted their donors to know how things were intertwined.

She called her assistant into her office. "Connie, who selects the menu?"

"The chef for the convention center's restaurant. We serve the standard choice of beef, chicken, or seafood. It has always been well received by the attendees. Are you thinking about changing it?"

"No, everything looks top-notch; I was just wondering where they purchase their food."

131

"I have no idea. May I ask why you care?"

She explained her idea about the theme being one of community. "I think it would be a nice touch if we provided foods and wines which were locally sourced. We may even want to encourage organically raised to promote a healthier lifestyle."

"It may cost more."

"Perhaps, but not significantly more. The example we're trying to set outweighs the cost."

"Do you want me to speak with the event planner for the convention center?" Connie asked.

"No, I'll take care of that. There is something else I'd like you to do. I'd like a video presentation to show during the dessert and coffee portion of the evening."

"We did that last year. I can put together the numbers and projections so they can see where their money is going."

Laurel shook her head. "That's not what I want. I want pictures of the children we have helped, video testimonials, and anything else which will personalize what we do. We could ask some of the pediatric oncologists if they have parents and patients who would like to help us. We would never infringe on their privacy—everything will be on a voluntary basis."

Connie became as enthusiastic as Laurel. "I know a videographer who would probably donate his time to do the filming and editing."

"Are you sure? We don't have a lot of time before the event. I know it would be a lot of work."

"The kind of crowd that will be in attendance is exactly the kind of people he'd like to have as clients. It would be worth it for him to do it at cost."

"Great. Call him and maybe David could speak

with some of the doctors for us."

Laurel made an appointment with the manager of the convention center and the restaurant's chef. She had initially been concerned they would be resistant to her ideas; however, they were pleasantly receptive. Convention centers try to capitalize on local attractions when groups or organizations visit the area. They considered it an experiment on someone else's budget. The chef called her a day later and told her they were fortunate that the area farmers were in the middle of fall harvest. He had no difficulty at all finding locally sourced vegetables and meat. When it was reasonable to do so, he was even able to obtain organically grown.

She took advantage of the autumn season, using that for the color scheme. The convention center was in capable hands with their management, making it one less thing she had to worry about. Then she called David. "Would you like to come over for dinner? I'm trying to bribe you."

He laughed. "How much you get out of me will depend on the meal. Is it a burger on the grill favor or pasta?"

"More like a standing rib roast."

"Sounds serious. I'll bring my appetite."

That evening he arrived with a bottle of wine and a playful kiss. "The table is set with candles; I can smell something that makes my mouth water. This looks more like a seduction scene."

She laughed as she handed him a glass of wine to relax while she was cooking. "You never know."

He took a sip of his wine. "What do you need?"

She filled him in on all the party details and left her request until the last. "Can you speak with some of the doctors and ask them if any of their patients and children would consent to give video testimonials for the hospital? Our foundation has funded so many programs and purchase of equipment, I want the patrons to see firsthand who it has helped."

"You went to all this expense and trouble for that? I'd be more than happy to speak with a few of the doctors I know. They get letters from families all the time, thanking them for saving their lives. You may even want to speak with Janet. I'm certain by now she has met many parents who are at various levels of treatment for their children."

"I had thought about that too, but Missy is in the preliminary stages of chemo and just lost all her hair. I was reluctant to ask her for anything."

"You don't have to ask her for anything. Just tell her what you are doing, and if she offers to help or give suggestions, let her. There is enormous comfort in speaking with others sharing your troubles."

"You're probably right, but I still feel like I might be stirring up some fears in her."

"I've seen her several times with both children, and that's not the impression I received. Perhaps you are overly sensitive because you know the family so well." Laurel nodded. "I'll call her tomorrow and see how things are going. I'll gauge her receptiveness by that. Come on," she said, pointing toward the kitchen. "I think your bribe is ready."

They had a delicious dinner and a pleasant evening. Laurel was tempted to ask him to stay but resisted. Instead, they listened to music while snuggling in front of the fireplace. It was a welcoming fire with the days becoming shorter and cooler with the autumn arriving.

At midnight he told her. "I think I had better get home. I'm on call all weekend."

She walked him to the door, they embraced, kissed, and she thanked him for the advice.

****

The following morning, Laurel called Janet. "How are things going?"

Janet's tone was more upbeat than she could remember in weeks. "Missy's home and doing well. We're going to keep her away from other children and any unnecessary exposure outside our house to reduce infection. Would you like to come over for coffee?"

Laurel was hesitant. "Are you sure you want me in the house?"

"Sometimes you must weigh the precautions with the psychological benefits. She knows not to climb all over people and why she must be careful—I'd love to see you."

"Okay, I'll be over in an hour."

She stopped by the bakery and bought some sweet rolls and two dozen of Missy's favorite cookies. When Janet let her in, the whole family was at home, and Laurel looked from one to other and started laughing. The only person who wasn't shaved bald was Janet.

Mike rubbed his son's head. "It's solidarity."

Missy came over to take the cookies from her and smiled broadly, completely at ease with the absence of her hair. When she and her brother went into the other room, Janet said, "Mike and MJ came to the hospital when she first lost her hair, and they had their heads shaved. It went a long way in making her feel better about it. The hospital gives the children a wide variety of hats for the kids to wear and then lets them decorate them any way they want."

"I think that's great. If there is ever anything you can think of that the foundation can provide, I'd be happy to look into it."

"How are the plans going for the fundraiser? I asked Harold Brennan if the bank would donate. I hope you don't mind, and that it's not a sore spot for you. They have been more than accommodating with me taking time off to be with Missy."

"Of course not. Harold is a good man, and if I had been asked by my superiors, I would have hand picked him as my replacement."

Janet gave Laurel a hug. "I knew you would never put any personal feelings you had above helping people through the foundation."

"I wanted to ask you something," Laurel began cautiously. "We're going to put together a video montage of children and their families who have been helped through the foundation and the hospital. Do you know any parents who might want to add their stories?" She touched Janet's arm. "I wasn't asking you to do it, just someone who has been through the process."

"We're too new to all of this, and I would be a little superstitious to add our story, but I know several people I could approach. Parents and their children become your new family. I treasure the new friendships even though the circumstances are tragic."

"Thank you. It would mean a lot. Have them contact my office. I want this to be the best event the foundation has ever given."

"With your energy and foresight, they couldn't have a better person in charge."

"I appreciate your confidence in me, but I think I

have been using this job to both distract and redeem myself. I haven't had time to brood over the past year."

"Who cares what your motivation is; it's the result that matters. We've all found ourselves outside our comfort zone at some point in our lives. I certainly never thought I'd have a child going through chemo and radiation treatments. The things in my life I've had to juggle sometimes blow my mind. I thank God every day that I have a loving supportive family and good friends like you. You have no idea how many people at the hospital have no one to lean on. I know of two examples where the couples have split up over the stress. Mike and I have become closer, but I'd be lying if I didn't tell you, it's been difficult."

Laurel smiled. "I'm so relieved that Missy is doing well."

"I know we are far from through this, but all the signs are on our side. I'm not complacent though we have to remain vigilant."

"Would you like to attend the dinner?"

Shaking her head, she said, "It's a worthy cause, but we just can't spare the money right now. With me on leave from work, Mike is working extra hours. It would be too much for us."

Laurel felt her friend could use a night out. "You'd be my guests. As you said, it is a worthy cause, and I know you need a night out especially one where you can see all that is being done for children like Missy."

Janet seemed to brighten at that. "Mike's parents wouldn't mind babysitting."

"Good, I'll make sure you have tickets, and I will give you updates on our progress putting it together."

Over the next few days, Laurel had updates on

parents and former patients who were more than willing to give testimonials. There were, in fact, so many they couldn't use all of them. She didn't want to disappoint any of the people who were so generous in giving of their time and personal struggles, so she found a compromise. The people who were not on the video presentation wrote personal testimonials. She printed all of them in a booklet to be distributed among the guests. There were pages of heartbreaking stories with positive outcomes. She was aware she was glorifying the success stories when there were many which were not. She did not want them to be forgotten, so for any family member who submitted a story where their child had succumbed, she had created a memorial page where they would be remembered.

****

A week before the event Laurel was feeling confident. There were none of the usual last-minute glitches. She and her assistant double and triple checked on every detail. She sent the final plan to Don Prentice for his stamp of approval.

"Laurel," he said, "I knew I picked the right person for this job. You're bringing back the heart to the foundation, and that's extremely important."

"You knew what you were doing when you made it personal. No one who had a personal relationship with a child battling leukemia could ever lose their heart. I've made it a point of visiting the hospital and hospitality homes we fund, and the people's reactions are much the same. They are all fearful but, more importantly, hopeful. It's the hope I want to build upon."

"I have such faith in you I sent a personal invitation to Dr. Norman to be my honored guest."

"Did he accept?"

The children's hospital had been courting Dr. Norman to head up the leukemia wing. If he came on board, deep-pocketed donors would follow. It was a longshot because the children's hospital was modest in comparison to the ones with whom he had been associated.

"He did. In fact, he said he wouldn't miss it."

Laurel knew this could be a defining moment for the hospital and the foundation, and she would do her best to capitalize on it.

Chapter Thirteen

Laurel wanted to share the good news with David, but the best she could do was exchange text messages. Flu season had begun, and it seemed as if every child in David's practice had been afflicted. He finally had time to call her.

"I'm so sorry," he said. "I don't know why parents wait until their kids get sick to concern themselves with flu shots. It's like locking the barn door after the horse escapes."

"I got mine if it makes you feel better," she teased.

"I'd love to see you, but honestly, I'm beat. I want to go for a run in the morning. Have you been to the cemetery recently?"

"Not since the swans migrated. I miss feeding them."

"Why don't you meet me there at eight, then I'll take you to breakfast. The trees and bushes are at their peak of autumn color and it's absolutely beautiful. I know you're not a runner, but we could do a brisk walk."

"I'd like that. I've been spending so much time at my office preparing for this fundraiser, I could use the fresh air. I need to have my brain aired out."

The next morning, she drove to the cemetery where he was already waiting for her in his car. She got out of her vehicle and pronounced, "It's a little chilly."

He gave her a kiss. "It won't seem so bad once we get walking."

"You're right, it is beautiful here," she said, and looked around, adding, "It seems there are several other walkers of the same opinion."

He reached for her hand as they walked through the crisp morning air. "There always are, the autumn brings more people here than any time of the year. Now tell me about the fundraiser."

She updated him about Dr. Norman.

"If he would consent to join the hospital staff, that would be a major coup," David said.

She nodded. "It would, but do you honestly think there is any chance of that? He consults at several of the major children's hospitals. I'm proud of what we have here, but it's not what he's used to having at his disposal. I'm afraid he won't take us seriously."

"That might be the reason he'd consider working at the hospital. He has a stellar reputation, and if he were to be given latitude to shape the leukemia unit, he might want to mold it into something special. The fact that he has even agreed to attend the fundraiser means he is interested and wants to work with you."

Laurel was excited at the prospect and asked, "Do you think so?"

Before he could answer, his phone rang. He looked at it and said, "Excuse me, it's my service. I know what this will mean."

He stepped a few feet away to take the call. "It isn't necessary to go to the Emergency Room. Send them to my clinic. I'm about fifteen minutes out." After clicking off, he glanced at her, looking sorry. "I need to I go. I'll walk you back to your car."

She shook her head. "Duty calls, I understand. I think I'll keep walking for a while. It's too nice of a day to spend inside, but you still owe me a meal."

He laughed. "Dinner tonight, I hope."

She watched as he sprinted back to his car while she continued her stroll. When she reached the top of the tallest driveway, she scanned the cemetery, taking in the beautiful trees, and smiled as the squirrels scampered about gathering nuts for the winter. She had a beautiful view of the pond where there were several ducks straggling behind. She wondered where they wintered when the pond froze over.

She was startled from her reverie when Maggie came up behind her. "Where have you been?" She sat on a monument which looked more like an engraved bench and patted it for Laurel to join her.

Laurel smiled. "Somehow it seems wrong to sit on someone's grave marker."

"That's why they chose a bench design. They want people to relax and take in the sights and sounds of the living."

Laurel gave an uneasy laugh and replied, "Too bad they can't enjoy the view."

"I'm certain they have a better view than most. So, to reiterate my question, where have you been?"

"Working."

Maggie nodded. "I read something about a big event coming up. Is that the organization you work for?"

Laurel nodded. "I'm in charge of it."

"Sounds impressive. You seem different from when I first met you. The work must agree with you."

Laurel took a deep breath and then exhaled. "It's

really satisfying to be able to do some good for others. It made me feel a little foolish over my own problems."

"Don't ever feel that way. We all have problems, and they help us grow."

"I certainly hope that has been the case. If you would like to go to the benefit, I could get you a ticket; I'm connected."

"Can I wear my pink bathrobe and fuzzy slippers?"

Laurel smiled at the image of Maggie showing up wearing them. "Only if you can add sequins to them; it's a black-tie affair."

"Then I'm out. What about that cute doctor? Is he going to be there?"

Laurel laughed. "I see you still have a one-track mind at matchmaking. He was just here with me, and to answer your question before you ask it, we've been seeing each other socially."

She snapped her fingers in glee. "I knew it. You're perfect for each other."

Laurel shook her head at the woman's insatiable desire to see her and David together. "You don't know either of us. How can you even say that?"

"I know more than you think. I can read between the lines. You were unhappy when we first met, and now, you're not. Isn't that all that matters?"

"I guess you're right. I haven't been dwelling on my problems like I did before."

Maggie cocked her head to one side as she asked in earnest, "Is it that you're not dwelling on your problems or have your problems gone away?"

Laurel stared at her, pondering the question she had never thought about. "To a considerable extent, I think my problems may have gone away. At the very least, they are on a sabbatical. Thank you for calling that to my attention."

Maggie giggled like a child. "What's a nosy old woman for?"

They said their goodbyes, and Laurel walked back to her car with a lighter step. She thought again about Maggie's question, and as she often did about things in her life, she analyzed it. It had been almost a year since her life, as she knew it, came crashing down. She had felt betrayed, confused, and lost.

The betrayal had lessened but would remain for a while longer, but she was no longer lost or confused. Moving into her childhood home had been the most important aspect of her healing. It was there she had the reinforcement of what held value. That value was in helping others. Once she had been distanced from Chaz's superficial quest for success, she was able to gain perspective. Her life had taken on a slower pace. Initially she thought that had been a bad thing. She had juggled a successful and often stressful career, and now she had turned that energy elsewhere. She found it ironic that a stranger seemed to know her better than she did herself.

When she returned home, she made a pot of coffee and pulled out her file for the fundraiser. She was satisfied with the itinerary for the evening. Don Prentice had wanted her to emcee the event, but she declined. He had been the founder of the charity, and it seemed only appropriate he be the master of ceremonies. He had a personality better suited for the job. Laurel tended to be understated in every aspect of her life and lacked his vibrato. He could be amazingly humorous with his self-deprecating humor and then instantly turn sentimental. She had attended events with him before when she was still at the bank, and more than once he had brought people to tears. It wasn't an act to raise funds, his devotion was genuine.

When he told her that Dr. Norman was attending, it added a new level of intensity on her part. She wasn't privy to his intentions, but she wanted to assure him and others the foundation was solidly behind the hospital and its outreach programs. She had added a couple of community program coordinators to the speakers list. There were groups who could give first-hand testimonials to the benefits of the foundation. As she was flipping through her lists, her phone rang.

"I thought you were at the office," David said, "but your assistant said you didn't come in."

"I decided to work here today. It's quieter without the constant phone ringing and fielding questions."

"I wanted to let you know that Janet and Mike took Missy back to the hospital. They called me and said she was running a fever and wanted to bring her to my office. Under the circumstances, I thought it was better for them to take her directly to the hospital. If it were serious, they would only have to go there anyway."

Into panic mode, Laurel dropped her files. "Will she be all right? Was there a relapse?"

"Relax, it's not uncommon and doesn't necessarily mean anything. Her resistance is low, but I didn't want to take a chance with her."

"I'll change and head to the hospital. They may need some moral support."

"Call me later," he said.

She headed directly for the hospital and found Janet and Mike in the waiting area. She was relieved to see they did not seem in distress. "What happened?"

Janet gave a weak laugh. "Overwrought parents. They said it wasn't anything serious. Her fever quickly subsided, and we are waiting to take her home."

Laurel dropped heavily into a chair next to them. "I'm so relieved."

"I'm glad you came, even though there was nothing you could do. I know how busy you are now, but your timing is perfect."

Smiling Laurel asked. "Why is that?"

Janet motioned for a young nurse to come over. "I want to introduce you to Colleen. She is a floor nurse in the unit and a leukemia survivor."

Laurel stood to shake her hand. "It's a real honor to meet you."

"The honor is mine. The Children's Leukemia Foundation helped to save my life. It was through your organization the hospital was able to purchase lifesaving equipment and therapeutics. Becoming a nurse was my way of repaying that gift."

Janet spoke up. "You had asked me if I knew of anyone who may be able to give you a testimonial. Here's your girl."

Laurel looked at Colleen. "Would you mind? I'd love to include you as a speaker. The fact that you are now a nurse in the very hospital that treated you is nothing short of inspirational."

"I would consider it a privilege."

Laurel took her name and phone number to contact her about the fundraiser.

"Isn't it odd how things worked out?" Janet said. "If we hadn't brought Missy in when we did, I wouldn't have met Colleen in time for the fundraiser."

"Sometimes I wonder if things are not just a coincidence."

Laurel waited around until Janet and Mike were ready to take Missy home. The little girl pranced out of the hospital as if she had just been to the shopping mall. It was a blessing that she could be so resilient. David had told her that many of the younger children never recall their treatments. She hoped that it was a memory Missy wouldn't have to revisit. It was bad enough her parents would never forget it.

When she was in her car before leaving the parking garage, she called David. "You should have seen the looks of relief on Janet and Mike's faces when Missy was discharged."

David hesitated a moment because he did not want to upset Laurel, but he warned her. "I'm glad it was nothing so they won't panic next time, because there will likely be a next time."

"That's just about the last thing I want to hear. I've been immersed in the literature enough to know you're right. It only makes me want to raise the foundation's profile even higher."

"I have no doubt you'll dazzle everyone. I even had my tuxedo dry-cleaned for the occasion."

She laughed. "I would hope so. I wouldn't want you to embarrass me with a dusty tuxedo."

"Oh, there are plenty of other ways I may embarrass you. I'm the world's worst dancer. I don't suppose you own steel-toed high heels?"

"I'll risk it."

"I generally avoid formal events, but I know the stakes are higher this year," he said.

"They are. If the foundation can impress Dr.

Norman and bring him on board with the hospital, it will be a game changer. A doctor of his stature brings high-profile donors."

"I have no illusions my presence would make a difference in your quest to lure him, but I will be by your side to help in any way I can."

She briefly told him about Colleen, and he agreed it would be an important addition. "When you can produce someone who has gone through the whole ordeal of treatment and a person who has decided to dedicate their life to help others, it will have a major impact."

She was slightly concerned about one aspect. "I thought the same thing. You don't think it's exploitive, do you?"

"Who cares? What if it is? It's not like it isn't true, and if she wants to share her experiences then I say—God bless her."

"You've got a point. I know if any of my bad experiences could help someone else, even if it is a cautionary tale, I'm okay with it."

There was pride in his voice. "Good girl. You're rising above your problems. We all need to do that."

She really wanted to hope he was right. He made everything easier just by being present. He never interfered with any of her decisions, offered advice only when it was asked for, and seemed to appreciate the same things she did. When she thought about Chaz, she realized that had been an important missing component in their marriage. He had a way of subtly manipulating her. He was always full of praise and kind words, which was warranted, but it was even more prevalent during social situations. She was his secret weapon, and she never knew it at the time. When trying to dazzle new or potential clients, he would entertain them with their wives or companions. Laurel was the perfect and gracious hostess, which helped to legitimize Chaz.

She was only now beginning to understand why her superiors at the banking conglomerate never embraced Chaz. They knew her and her reputation before she met Chaz. After he disappeared, her former bosses had been free with their opinion of him when speaking to her.

"I think it would be better if you met me at the convention center the night of event. I'll bring my clothes with me and change there because I might need to tweak a few things at the center."

"You mean micromanage, don't you?"

"Not at all. The staff at the convention center are topnotch and seem to have everything under control. I have been the beneficiary of the planning which went into the past events. Connie has been invaluable in advising me with what worked and what could use improvement."

There may have been some truth to her pronouncement, but she was not giving herself the well-deserved credit. The convention center staff were seasoned professionals at preparing banquets. The food would be excellent, the service first rate, and everything would run smoothly. That was the mechanics of any banquet; Laurel gave it its own heart. Her autumn theme brought warmth and comfort to the impersonal banquet hall. She carried that through to the programs she designed. She left no one out from the hospital administrator to the organic farmer who donated the produce. She believed in all facets of life there are moving parts. One small break and it could bring down the entire system. It was a metaphor she wanted to apply to their fundraising efforts.

Before ending their conversation, David said, "I know how important the success of the event is to you. If you need anything at all, let me know, even if it's just to hear your thoughts aloud."

She felt his sincerity and was grateful for his steadying friendship and sound judgement.

Chapter Fourteen

The day of the fundraiser finally arrived. A couple of hours before the beginning of the festivities, Laurel conferred with the staff, going over seating charts, checking microphones, and making certain the bar was well stocked. Her assistant Connie was in attendance to check on things, but she was already dressed in her gown when she pointed to the clock. "You had better change, Laurel. Things start in a half hour."

Laurel laughed. "You don't think the jeans would be a hit?"

"Come on, I'll help you. Don't forget you are the conductor of this symphony."

Laurel used the convention center's dressing room to change into her dress. In keeping with the fall colors, she'd chosen taffeta gown in burnt orange. Since it had been a long time when she'd had the necessity to dress for a formal function, she was afraid she was out of practice. She turned in a circle for inspection.

Connie giggled. "I could never get away with a dress like that; I'd look like a plump over-ripe pumpkin."

"You would not. You have a lovely figure."

"It doesn't matter. My husband agreed to take me for better or worse."

Connie left the dressing room, then popped her head back. "There is a gentleman straight off the cover of GQ waiting for you."

Laurel stepped out into the hallway and found David waiting. He approached, both arms extended. "You're breathtaking."

She walked into his arms for a kiss. "It doesn't look like you were picking out of garbage cans either."

Taking her hand, he led her into the ballroom. "A few people are starting to wander in; you had better make your presence known."

Most of the people at the event were not personally known to her, but when given their names, she instantly knew who they were and greeted each warmly. David gravitated between Laurel and some of the doctors he was acquainted with and waved her over. "This old reprobate claims to know you."

"Dr. Joe!" she exclaimed, giving him an enormous hug. "I can never thank you enough for all the care you gave my mother."

With a touch of sadness in his voice, he said, "I'm just sorry I couldn't have done more for her."

"You of all people know her heart had been failing her for years," Laurel reminded him. "It always amazed me how well she did, living all by herself."

"When you moved back home, it took an incredible amount of pressure off her."

"I'm happy she never had to experience my downfall," she told him, fully aware he must have known about it.

"I'd hardly call this a downfall. What you've put together is nothing short of spectacular. I could have used your energy and expertise before I retired from the heart-fund drive. Your mother was relentless with her contribution."

Surprised, Laurel said, "My mother?"

"You didn't know? That was just like her to stay in the background. She coordinated teams who collected for the Heart Association."

All Laurel could do was shake her head with a smile and answer. "She never said a word."

David had been listening intently. "You never told me your mother had heart issues, only that she had been in ill health and died."

Laurel never thought her omission was important. "I never thought about it."

"It doesn't matter, but I was wondering if she and my mother had ever met. My brother's heart condition spurred her to donate her time as well."

Dr. Joe chimed in. "It's entirely possible they crossed paths, but there are so many parts to the annual heart drive and awareness program, they may not have met." He was then summoned away by a former colleague, leaving David and Laurel alone.

"Wouldn't that have been an amazing coincidence if they knew each other?" he asked.

"It certainly would have been. Your mother died a few years before mine; maybe my mother even went to her funeral service."

"Honestly," he began, "there were so many people I didn't know who attended I couldn't even begin to remember. She touched many lives in pursuit of helping families like ours with sick children."

Laurel slid one arm around his waist. "Let's just pretend they did know each other. We can then call our meeting fate."

"Works for me."

The waiters and waitresses supplied endless hors

d'oeuvres and glasses of the finest local wines to the willing guests. Don Prentice took Laurel's arm and introduced her to the deep-pocket donors. He made a point of telling everyone she was the architect of evening and had her finger on everything the foundation needed to help the community. She was thankful she had studied up on many of the people Don was introducing her to and had a working knowledge of their business and interests.

A voice from behind said, "Good evening, Mrs. Tanner."

She thought her breath had left her when she turned to face Robert Durant, the man from whom Chaz purchased his company along with the naming rights.

She took a deep breath to maintain her composure and replied, "Good evening, Mr. Durant. It was kind of you to attend."

She hadn't seen his name on the list, or she would have been prepared for the awkward encounter. He may have been a guest of a patron of whom she would have no knowledge and no way to prepare herself for his attendance.

"Where is your husband this evening?" he asked, sarcasm clear in his voice.

"I assume you are referring to my ex-husband, and your guess would be as good as mine. And my name is Quincy," she said with an authority she did not feel.

A waiter passed by Durant, who grabbed a glass of wine from the tray before answering. "What's in a name? A rose or whatever Shakespeare said—oh, I know—the total destruction of someone's reputation that took a lifetime to build."

Laurel was aware Mr. Durant took a beating to his

good name because Chaz had bought his name with the company. The man, like herself, had been maligned for something beyond his control.

"I'm deeply sorry for the position Chaz put you in, but you were never defrauded out of a dime. He paid you what you asked for your business."

He raised his voice loud enough to attract the attention of those around them. "Do you think it's all about money? My clients trusted me; consequently they trusted your husband. There are circles in which my name is Mudd."

In a hushed but firm tone she replied, "Join the club."

Don Prentice interrupted. "What's going on here? People are staring."

"I've known you for thirty years, Don, and I can't believe you'd let the fox in the hen house," the man said. "Have you taken leave of your senses?"

Don used a voice Laurel had never heard from him. "You're out of line, Durant. Laurel Quincy has been as much a victim as anyone else, including and especially you. You saw a good deal, and you took it. Don't blame anyone else. Right now you have two choices: stay and appreciate the importance of this evening in the lives of needy children or you can leave."

Robert Durant said no more, but he was still angry. Don gave Laurel a fatherly look. "Are you okay?"

She nodded. "I just need a few minutes to recoup. Please excuse me."

She headed for the dressing room, brushing by David without looking at him. He tried to say something to her, but Don motioned him over. "Durant is here; he was less than gentlemanly with Laurel."

155

"Okay, I'll take care of it."

He didn't let propriety stand in his way. He walked directly into the dressing room where he found her. She was sitting on a stool in front of a large mirror with her head resting in her hands. She didn't look at him but said, "I don't suppose you're in here to touch up your makeup."

He pulled out a stool to sit next to her. "I think I can say the same of you."

She turned to look at him. She hadn't been crying because the hurt was too deep for tears. "I thought I was past this. Will I ever be free?"

He put his hand on hers and said, "If you want to be. Durant is feeling not unlike yourself. Was he out of line? Hell, yes, he was, but I think you can understand that. This may happen again, but time is your friend in circumstances such as these."

"What if he is saying things that might stop people from donating? I can take anything for myself, but not for the foundation. Too much is riding on these grants and donations."

Speaking sternly, he said, "I want you to remember something; you are not Laurel Tanner, you are Laurel Quincy, a woman with no past indiscretions, real or imagined. She is kind and decent, filled with love and charity. The woman who is going to go back out there on my arm."

"Laurel." Connie dashed into the room, looking first at her boss, then at David. "What are you doing in here?"

"I got the wrong restroom."

Waving her hand, she said, "Whatever." She turned to Laurel. "Dr. Norman has arrived. Mr. Prentice wants you front and center."

David stood up, took Laurel's hand. "Showtime, my dear."

They found their way to Mr. Prentice and Dr. Norman. Pleasantries were exchanged, and Dr. Norman said, "You've put together an impressive event. I'll be looking forward to the presentation."

"We're honored to have you with us," she said. "Any suggestion you could offer would be greatly appreciated."

Laurel and Mr. Prentice had decided to do the presentation during the dessert portion of the evening. They wanted to ply their guests with a gourmet meal and drinks before appealing to their humanitarian side. She had placed a simple speaker's dais with a large screen behind it for the video presentation. Mr. Prentice would have a remote control to change the images or play select videos during his speech.

Laurel seated the hospital administrator next to Dr. Norman at the same table with herself, David, Don, and Mrs. Prentice. They wanted to gauge Dr. Norman's reaction and give him a chance to speak with the administrator. The Children's Leukemia Foundation was a separate entity from the hospital, but their major focus had been on providing as much financial assistance as possible.

After finishing their meal, the dessert and coffee was being served when Don proceeded to the dais. He performed the obligatory remarks of appreciation for everyone who had attended before starting his presentation. "I want to let others show you the importance of your donation. They can speak for themselves better than anything I could say."

He then went ahead to play photos and videos of touching success stories from both patients and their families. Person after person expressed their gratitude for the support of the foundation and the hospital. Their testimonials left many in the room in tears.

Don stopped the video and said, "I'd now like to ask our honored speakers to give their firsthand accounts of their experiences."

A little girl stepped forward being accompanied by her parents. They held her up to the microphone and she bubbled enthusiastically about how the hospital, and all the doctors and nurses who helped her get better. She was no longer sick, and she wanted everyone to know that. The room burst into applause, and the little girl giggled with pleasure. Her father could be heard saying, "Good job, honey," as they led her off the dais.

She was followed by several other parents and children of all ages who were able to better articulate their experiences and successful cures. The final speaker was Colleen, the young nurse Laurel had only just met. Her story was the most poignant. She had been able to not only relate her own childhood battle with leukemia but how it had inspired her to give back by becoming a nurse. The compassion and sincerity in her story left chills running up and down Laurel's spine, and she was certain she was not the only one. When the young woman finished speaking, the room was momentarily silent before she received a standing ovation. She gave a simple wave and left. She did not want to make the evening too personal.

Don replaced her at the podium. "Please reach into your wallets and help us, help them. If you know of anyone who cannot give monetarily, we could always use volunteers both at the foundation and the hospital." He continued. "Before I end this evening, I'd like to ask Laurel Quincy to stand for acknowledgment. This event would not have been possible without her dedication, imagination, and unique abilities. Please join me with a round of applause."

The room clapped almost as joyfully as they had after the little girl's testimonial. Laurel was embarrassed as David whispered, "Take a bow, you've earned it."

She turned toward the crowd and briefly bobbed her head before sitting down. She leaned into David and said, "I hope it has all been worth it."

The evening was not over after the presentations; there was dancing and another round of hors d'oeuvres, as if anyone could eat another thing. It had been Laurel's plan to keep the guests there after the speeches so they could mingle with the donors and receive some feedback. She saw Robert Durant approaching.

"Laurel, I owe you my deepest apologies. I let our personal history cloud my judgement. You have done a beautiful job for the foundation, and I want to personally give you my check."

He pulled his checkbook from his inner pocket and wrote a check for ten thousand dollars and handed it to her. She looked at it in awe. "I don't know what to say. This is very generous of you, both financially and personally."

"I like to think I'm man enough to admit when I've been wrong. Don was right about you being the person to lead this initiative. Providence put you here. Keep up the good work."

"That means a lot, thank you."

David took her out on the dance floor and held her close as they moved across the room. "That was exactly what you needed to hear. He must be a good man, deep inside."

"I don't think it's too deep. I've never heard anyone say an unkind thing about him. He was just hurt in another way."

As they were dancing, David received a tap on his shoulder for someone asking to cut in. It was Dr. Norman. "May I?" he asked.

David replied with levity, "Just remember where you got her."

"It's been a lovely evening," Dr. Norman said.

"I know I've thanked you before, but it bears repeating; thank you for being here."

"I've spent a great deal of time with your hospital administrator. He's trying to woo me to head the research department."

"Is he being successful?"

"I've been content at the University Hospital I've been at for the last ten years."

With a tone of disappointment. "Then that's a no?"

"I don't want to settle for contentment because it is akin to complacency. I need a challenge. You have a nice hospital, but it could use some innovation."

"I didn't think we were that archaic. Our foundation stays abreast of the latest technology and therapies. We've largely been limited by funding. We have applied for some substantial matching grants. That's what tonight was about."

He hoped she wasn't offended when she had misunderstood his meaning. "It wasn't my intention to minimize your efforts. The hospital here has many things going for it, from geographical proximity to other major hospitals to community enthusiasm. Tonight certainly proved that, and I'm looking for just that passion and support. I've had a long and largely successful career, but I want to end it with a worthwhile commitment to making a difference. People in the research field mistakenly believe that they need a grand discovery to be relevant. I've seen more progress from accumulative research. I want to expand on that, and the children's hospital here is the place to do that."

She stopped dancing to look into his eyes. "Then you are going to accept the administrator's offer?"

"We have some details to work out, but the short answer is yes."

She was nearly busting with enthusiasm. "You have no idea what this will mean to our community."

He shook his head. "I'm not a one-man band. I don't want to give you any false expectations. Don't expect miracles. Medicine is often a process with a lot of trial and error."

"That may be true, but it all comes with hope, and hope is what we all cling to in times of trouble. Have you told Mr. Prentice?"

He turned her around just in time to see Don Prentice dancing a jig. "I guess that would be yes."

Chapter Fifteen

The evening ended. Laurel and Don thanked the guests personally as they left. Don and his wife, along with David and Laurel, were the only people present when a waiter came to their table with a bottle of champagne.

"Who ordered this?" Laurel asked.

David replied, "I did. I think you and Don have earned it."The cork was popped, and the waiter filled their glasses as the rest of the staff started cleaning up the room. They clinked glasses for a job well done.

"I don't think I have ever been this tired," Laurel said. "When Robert Durant first approached me, I thought the whole evening was over. Funny how things can turn around."

David said, "You look like you could fall asleep right here. Would you like me to drive you home? I don't want you to fall asleep at the wheel."

"My body is tired, but my mind is still racing with all kinds of ideas and scenarios. I won't fall asleep."

Don Prentice offered, "I'll pay for a room for the night at the convention center hotel for you. My wife and I only live a short distance from here or I'd do the same thing."

"Thanks, but no. I want to crash in my own bed."

David said, "I'll follow you home, and we'll get together later tomorrow."

Laurel was correct when she said her mind was racing. She could not have been more pleased with how everything turned out. She was, however, very curious as to the donation total. It would be at least a week before she would know. Not everyone, like Mr. Durant, wrote a check on the spot. Don had told her the reason he held the fundraiser near the end of the year had to do with wealthy donors wanting to use it as a tax deduction. Usually, they had a reasonable idea of their yearly net by that time, and donations were given accordingly. The upcoming holidays were also an incentive.

Laurel pulled into her driveway with David behind her. He rolled down his window, and she stuck her head in to kiss him goodnight. "No one could have asked for a more handsome and gracious escort."

"It was entirely my pleasure. You had better get inside, Cinderella. It's past midnight."

She laughed. "Are you afraid my dress will turn into rags?"

"No, I'm afraid I'll turn into a frog."

"But a well-dressed one."

****

Laurel was having her coffee when David called the next morning. "Did you read the paper?"

"I'm barely awake," she said. "I haven't even gone out to get it."

"There is a picture of you and Don in the local section. It had a nice write-up about the fundraiser."

"How could they have gotten the story ready so quickly?"

"They probably had most of it written beforehand and tweaked it a bit and added the photo. Maybe it will bring in more donations."

"We did prepare a press release so maybe they used that."

****

A few days later, her doorbell rang, and she found her attorney Stuart Hoffman standing there. She hadn't spoken with him since he sent her the divorce papers. Her first reaction was one of concern. Things were going so well she didn't want anything to disrupt her life.

"Is something wrong?"

"Not this time. May I come in?"

She pulled the door wider and replied, "Certainly, forgive my bad manners. I just made a fresh pot of coffee. Would you care for a cup?" He had just told her it wasn't bad news, but she couldn't imagine what would prompt his visit.

He followed her into the kitchen and made himself comfortable at the table. She filled his mug with coffee and placed a plate of cookies in front of him. He paused from his mission long enough to take advantage of both. "Your former employers have asked me to speak with you. They were more than a little impressed with how you have managed to bounce back after everything that has happened to you in this past year."

"How would they know that?" she asked while filling her own mug.

"The local papers were not the only newspapers to cover the charity event. The Bridgefield branch and its sister banks are patrons, so they were kept informed. At the time of your dismissal, they told you they still believed in you. They were only waiting for the scandal to calm down."

"That's all in the past. I know why they had to do it, and they were more than generous. There are no hard feelings."

"You have somehow managed to avoid any stigma being attached to you. I personally believe it's because you've always been transparent. I helped you through this, and I know what a blow it was to you—you kept your head and self-respect."

"I thank you for the compliment, but it was really more about 'do I want to sink or swim.' "

"It looks like you're swimming just fine."

Basic curiosity made her probe into his intentions. "I don't think you have come here to learn about my swimming lessons."

"Corporate has asked me to speak with you about returning to the company."

"A job offer? Why did they send you?"

"They thought I was the logical choice to feel you out about returning. I was the one they sent to help you navigate the whole Chaz debacle, and they knew we had a rapport."

"Exactly what are they offering me?"

"Similar to what you were doing here originally only on a national level. They would like you to return to New York where you would work directly under Tom Underwood leading the new acquisitions of merging banks."

He nearly left her breathless. Not only were they offering her a job but a substantial promotion, even from the position she held when she was in New York. She was certain she misunderstood him. "You aren't serious?"

"Dead serious. This would put you back on track to

where you were before you ever met Chaz."

She was still dumbstruck. "I don't even know how to respond to that."

"I understand, and they don't need an immediate answer. If you are receptive to taking the job, they will send over all the information concerning the position and salary. You can have until the beginning of the new year. Sometime in January they would like an answer. That should give you plenty of time to think it over."

"Naturally, I'm interested, but I have many things to consider. This has taken me completely off guard. Despite corporate's claim they never lost faith in me, I never expected they would ask me to return."

"They understand that and even anticipated you would carefully weigh your options. For what my opinion is worth, I think it's where you belong."

There was a long silence between them. When she finally spoke, she asked, "Have you heard anything about Chaz?"

"When I sent you your divorce papers, I closed any inquiry on him. I had hoped you had, too. That's a dead end for you, Laurel. I think you should avoid going there."

"Oh, I have. But can you understand my curiosity? He was, after all, my husband."

He stood up to leave. "You know what they say about curiosity and the cat."

"Point taken."

She felt like she was riding a roller coaster and did not know if it would go off its rail. The year had begun with betrayal, humiliation, and unemployment. It was now ending with the potential of exceeding any career goals she had imagined. She needed to figure out if that's what she wanted. All her reasons for wanting it no longer existed, but did she want it for herself?

David called and texted her several times, but she did not answer him. She was still processing the amazing offer she had been given and how to discuss it with him. Finally, she called him and asked if he could come over.

"Is everything all right? You sound stressed."

She reassured him she was fine, but it was complicated. He said he would be over right after he saw his last patient. When he arrived, Laurel had the fireplace blazing and a bottle of wine chilled. She ushered him to the sofa, patted the cushion for him to sit beside her, and handed him a glass of wine.

"This doesn't look like unwelcome news, but I'm not so sure."

"My lawyer was here today."

He shook his head. "I wasn't aware you had one."

"I told you about him. He's the guy the bank sent to represent me and processed my divorce."

"Okay, but why was he here?"

"My old bosses want me back with a huge promotion and salary increase."

"If that's what you want, I'm thrilled for you. You could take the job and still offer your assistance to the foundation. If the money is that substantial, you could work pro bono. That would be a win-win."

"Not exactly."

"Why?"

"The job is back in New York City."

He stared at her. "Are you going to take it?"

"Honestly, I don't know."

"What about all the stuff you told me about losing

your job may have been a blessing in disguise—that you were doing something important, that it gave you a new perspective. Were you kidding yourself or me?"

She tried to calm him. "David, please; I'm trying to be upfront with you."

He was clearly angry. "Like you were being up front when you told me you didn't know if you still loved Chaz?"

She was now irritated. "This is not the same thing. I've made no decision, but I'd be a fool not to weigh all the options."

He stood up slamming his wine glass down nearly breaking it. "Am I one of those options? I thought we were headed toward something meaningful."

She stood up too and reached for his hand, but he pulled it away. "You are the most important consideration in all of this. There may be a compromise somewhere in this."

"What compromise could there be if you are in New York and I'm here?"

"I don't know; that's why I'm weighing everything carefully. It's necessary for you to understand I have worked for a moment like this my whole life. My parents sacrificed for it."

He grabbed his coat and headed for the door but turned to ask her. "And where are your parents now?"

"David," she called to him. The only sound she heard was the door slamming shut.

****

She did not sleep much that night. The question he'd posed—"where are your parents now?"—echoed in her head. She felt no better the next day and wandered around her house until she was stir-crazy.

She grabbed her coat and headed for her car. It was cold and an occasional snowflake tried to stick to the ground but there was no accumulation. When she left the house, she thought she had no specified direction in mind, but she found herself at the cemetery. She drove up the lane to where her parents were buried.

She sat down on the ground in front of their headstone and said aloud, "I wish you were here to guide me. I seem to keep messing everything up."

She heard a voice behind her and intuitively knew it was Maggie, even hoping it was her. She looked up to see the old woman snuggled in a warm parka and boots. "You'll freeze in these temperatures, child."

"I didn't plan ahead."

She had a soothing tone in her voice. "Looks like you're asking your parents for advice."

Laurel sighed. "They are remarkably silent."

"I wouldn't be so sure about that."

Laurel almost grunted when she asked, "Do you know something I don't?"

"Nope," she said in a short reply and continued. "Everything they'd tell you; you already know."

"You don't even know why I'm here."

"Doesn't matter; the answer would be the same. I have only learned a little about you over the past few months of running into you here, but I'm a fairly good judge of character. I suspect you had loving and devoted parents, and they aptly prepared you for everything in life. Maybe not anything specific, but the core to all your answers is there."

Laurel felt the woman had years of wisdom to offer her. "How do I access them?"

Maggie touched her coat where her heart was.

"First you listen to that"—she tapped her head—"then to that."

It sounded simple enough, but there was a painful process to it. She returned home for some soul searching and decided what she had to do.

****

David was at his clinic seeing patients but barely communicating with his nurse. At the end of the day, she came into his office. "You have an unscheduled patient in room four."

He was tired and just wanted to go home and be miserable in peace. "Who is it?"

"Someone new."

Annoyed, he snapped, "Tracy, you know I don't like to see new patients at the end of day. I want more time to go over the charts and evaluate them."

"Deal with it."

He went into room four where he found Laurel sitting on the exam table. David's nurse whispered, "I'm going home."

He smiled at Laurel. "What seems to be your problem?"

"It's my eyesight," she replied somberly. "I can't seem to see what's right in front of me." She slid off the table and into his arms. "I'm sorry, Laurel, I was out of line. It was like déjà vu."

"No, you weren't. It was different this time. We were only just getting to know each other when we had our first misunderstanding. We can't run out on each other when we have to talk things through. You basically called me out as a hypocrite; you weren't wrong. I said those things about wanting something different, and I thought I meant them."

In a discouraged tone, he asked, "And you didn't?"

"That's what I want to tell you—I did mean them; I just had to process this unexpected offer. I'm not going to take the job offer. I'm not that person any longer, but I'm also not a fool. I want to leave my options open with them in the event something comes my way that fits into both our lives. I worked hard to get where I was, and I don't want to throw away my relationship with corporate."

"I can respect that. What brought you to this conclusion?"

"You said something to me which touched a nerve. You asked, 'where are my parents now?' and I had to answer that question."

He was remorseful for his unkind words. "I was angry and hurt and should never have said that."

"It was a wake-up call. I went to the cemetery and that old woman Maggie was there. I didn't tell her any of the story, but she told me that whatever was troubling me I already knew the answer. She was right. My parents would want me to live for myself, not some notion I may have of what they would want for me. I don't need a six-figure income to be happy. I've never had expensive tastes and I'm content with my work at the foundation. That's not to say I may not do something else, but it would be within the same life parameters. Right now, I need to grasp with both hands the things I do have, and the main one is you."

He held her close. "That's all I needed to hear. Let's get out of this place."

****

They spent their first night together since the night of the storm. Neither wanted the morning to come, but eventually daylight found its way. Laurel slipped out of bed, made coffee, and brought a cup to him so he wouldn't have to get out of bed.

He sat up and asked, "What, no bacon and eggs?"

She slid back beneath the covers. "Don't push your luck."

"I woke up next to you; that's all the luck I need."

"What time do you have to be at the clinic?"

He looked over at the clock. "Not for a while yet. What about you?"

"That's the wonderful thing about my job. I can work here or go into the office. I should probably go to the office. I'm waiting for the final tally from the donors, or at least a rough estimate. I want to know if we hit the amount we need for some matching grants."

He hesitated a moment before speaking. "At the risk of bringing up a sore subject, what are you going to tell your old bosses?"

She snuggled against his chest. "I've been thinking about that. I don't want to alienate them. I want to keep channels open for a variety of reasons, including help with the foundation. They are an enormous entity which only keeps growing in a variety of areas. If I'm honest and straightforward with them, it would only be to my benefit. Don't worry if I'm still on track with our understanding."

"I'm not worried; at least not any longer."

Laurel crafted a diplomatic e-mail, praising the company and expressing her gratitude for the generous offer, but she needed to decline. She cited personal issues and, without going into detail, said she was available if they ever needed a consultation. She was certain she left the door open for other opportunities.

Chapter Sixteen

Laurel was at her desk when her assistant brought her a stack of mail, most of it from donors. "Grab a letter opener, and let's see what we got," Laurel said.

One by one, they ripped them open. Occasionally Laurel or Connie would say, "Not bad from so and so," or "I was really expecting more from Mr. and Mrs. XYZ." It was the check from Marcus Petroski that stunned both: a check for two million dollars. Laurel's hand was nearly shaking when she handed the check to Connie. "I'm not questioning the donation, but what would possess him to give such a large amount?"

"I thought you knew."

"Knew what?"

"Colleen Kennedy is his granddaughter. I assumed that's why you asked her to speak."

Laurel shook her head. "She never said anything. Her speech touched everyone's heart."

"Quite possibly that may have been the point. Why don't you personally thank him," Connie suggested.

"For two million, I'd give him my right arm."

"I'll get you his office address," Connie said and promptly returned with it written on a notepad.

Laurel had expected a sizable donation from him because he had been generous in the past, but she certainly did not expect so much. Marcus Petroski had been a self-made man in the technology industry, was known for his philanthropy. His office was only a few blocks away, so she promptly went to thank him. Knowing his great wealth, she had expected an opulent suite of offices, but it had been quite modest. Everything was high-end but understated. In her tenure with the bank, she had visited many multi-million, even billion-dollar businesses that flaunted their wealth for show. Mr. Petroski was not one of those people.

She asked the receptionist if he was available, and much to her surprise, he came out personally to greet her. "Ms. Quincy, please come in."

Laurel glanced around the room, and it was filled with photos. "Your family?"

He was obviously proud of them by the way he beamed. "All four children, their spouses, and sixteen grandchildren."

He took down a photo and handed it to Laurel. "I believe you'll recognize this one."

It was Colleen at her college graduation in the same frame as a photo of her in the hospital as a child. Laurel felt compelled to clarify her visit. "Mr. Petroski, the foundation cannot thank you enough for your donation, however I must tell you I honestly did not know Colleen's connection to you. I don't want you to think I tried to exploit her for gain."

He stopped her from continuing by putting up his hand. "I know that. It's the reason my donation was two million, not my usual two hundred thousand. Don Prentice has done many remarkable things with the foundation, but it didn't take me long to recognize you have given it a new energy. Making it more of a community badge of honor touched me. When you have watched a child suffer and you don't know from one day to next how long you will have that child, it changes you. I found out how little anything beyond that young life mattered. Have you ever experienced such a thing?"

"I know the helplessness of not being able to save a loved one, but not a child. That puts a whole new spin on things. My dear friend's daughter is now undergoing leukemia treatments at the hospital. It was in no small part the reason that I accepted this position."

"A tragedy is only a tragedy if no good can come from it. Your friend's child will have brought help to countless children through you and the foundation. I learned that from Colleen. It's not supposed to be the correct thing to admit, but she is my favorite grandchild. She was a brave little fighter for herself and now for others. She has a big heart."

"I suspect she's not the only one."

"Ms. Quincy, we all have a place and purpose in this world. I do not have the knowledge or skill of a doctor, but my skills have supported me amply. My contribution must be money to those who have those skills. The presentation I observed the other night convinced me you will use it to the best advantage. I don't even know you, but I'm a good judge of character."

She was humbled. "I have recently been struggling with my purpose; thank you for validating my choices."

"You're more than welcome. Just give me more Colleens, and we can save the world."

Laurel stood and shook his hand. "I'll do my best."

Mr. Petroski's contribution put the fundraising donations over the top, qualifying them for the much-needed grants. Don was so overwhelmed he offered to give her a raise.

"I can't believe I'm saying this, but I don't need one. Money is nice to have, but for the time being I want every dollar to go into the foundation. We can revisit this subject at another time."

****

The Thanksgiving holiday was creeping up, and Laurel was painfully aware it would be the first holiday season since her divorce. When her mother was alive, she celebrated with her and Chaz with a quiet dinner but still honoring all the traditions. In years past, when she was unable to return home to Rose Hill, her mother had volunteered at the hospitality houses for the hospital. Ill health prevented her from doing so in the final years of her life. After her death, Laurel and Chaz were invited to a client's house to dine where she would bring a contribution from her family holiday menu. This year she wasn't sure what to do.

When she asked David, he had a suggestion. "It's been years since I've had a family Thanksgiving. What would you think about me inviting my brother and his family? He hasn't been home since our mother's death, and I seldom get a chance to see my niece and nephew. I have plenty of room at my place. They could stay with me, and you could help me with the dinner. Unless you think it's an imposition."

"I'd love that. Do you think they would come?"

"A simple phone call will give us that answer."

He picked up the phone, and she waited as he spoke to him. "Hey, little brother, what would you say about bringing your family here for Thanksgiving? There is someone I'd like you to meet."

Laurel couldn't hear the other end of the

conversation, but the gist of it was brotherly taunting. There was silence for a few minutes while David put his hand over the receiver and told her, "He's checking with his wife."

David said into the phone, "Great, bring nothing but your appetite. I have plenty of room for all of you, and you can stay for as long as you can stand me."

He was giddy when he told her they were coming. "I don't know why I didn't do this before."

"You were still grieving for what might have been. I'm certain he realized that, and I'd be willing to bet he had extended an invitation to you in the past."

David shook his head. "He did and while I always knew I was welcome any time, I wasn't ready. What about you?"

"I want to make new traditions, but I'd like to bring a few of my childhood ones with me. Since my mom died, Chaz and I let tradition get away from us."

David had been a bachelor for a long time. His house was neat, tidy, and cleaned regularly by a cleaning service, but it lacked intimacy. It was far too large for a single man, but he had bought it prior to his broken engagement. Laurel wasn't crass enough to ask, but she was certain it was in anticipation of having children.

"I'm going to need your help. I want to get this place child-friendly ready. I would like the kids to be comfortable."

Sarcastically she quipped, "Give me a break. Who knows more about children than a pediatrician? I've seen you fake it by asking them about the latest video games or clothing trends. How old are your niece and nephew?"

"Tina is six and Drew is eight."

"So, we're talking dolls, race cars, and age-appropriate video games."

"I guess."

She started laughing. "Your mission, should you choose to accept it, is to quiz every child coming through your door. I'm more out of touch than you are."

Laurel's suggestion was brilliant; not only did he get some valuable information, but the kids were so distracted by his questions they didn't mind being examined.

After each one left, he quickly jotted down ideas and pawned them off on Laurel.

She flipped through the list and asked with amusement. "Did it ever occur to you to simply ask your brother?"

"Are you crazy? Do you think for one moment I'd let him think I didn't know what I was doing? I love my brother, but I'd never live it down."

Laurel almost choked with laughter. "This is what I missed as an only child—no one to blackmail."

Laurel had been to David's house many times but never had a reason to explore it. He had bedrooms for everyone, but they were generically decorated. It was inexpensive for her to buy children's comforters for their beds and whimsical posters and nightlights. She and David went to an electronics store and bought the latest gaming system and video games he felt comfortable were appropriate. He had become somewhat of an expert on that subject. He treated many children addicted to them and was careful in his selections. They also discussed other activities which would get them outdoors.

Laurel was both nervous and excited about meeting David's family. She had several cousins, but they did not live in the immediate area, and she was starting to feel that lack of family. If she could be part of his, she hoped it would fill the void and add a new dimension to their relationship.

****

His brother and family arrived in the late afternoon before Thanksgiving. It did not make sense for them to fly, but it was an eight-hour drive from Boston. The children were kept occupied with movies on DVD, so it minimized the long trip.

Laurel was there to greet them when the kids scrambled out of the car for a hug from their uncle. David put his arm around Laurel's waist. "I'd like you to meet Laurel Quincy. This poor excuse for a human being is my brother, Tim, his wife, Cara, and the rambunctious Tina and Drew."

They exchanged handshakes and headed for the house. David and Tim led the way, and all Laurel heard were insults and laughs. Cara stopped Laurel from following too close behind and said, "They both need this. Thank you."

Laurel wasn't totally informed on all the nuances between the brothers. "This was David's idea; I'm just helping."

"It never occurred to him before. He is a good man, and he's been very hurt. He is now the man I remember, and that's because of you."

Laurel didn't want to divulge too much information to a stranger so blanketed her response. "We understand each other."

David, uncertain as to what time they might arrive,

decided ordering pizza was the best meal choice. The kids grabbed sodas and slices of pizza and disappeared into the family room to watch videos while the adults chatted. Laurel and Cara listened indulgently as the brothers told stories, shared inside jokes, and did a lot of back slapping.

"Were they always like this?" Laurel asked.

With a bemused look on her face Cara replied, "Sadly, this is the tamed-down version."

Laurel shook her head in mirth. "I've never seen him this happy. Did you grow up with them?"

"No, Tim and I met at college, but we came back to his parents' home whenever possible."

"So, you knew his parents?" Laurel asked wanting to know more about David's life.

"Yes, but I didn't get a chance to know his father for very long. He was a laid-back, self-effacing, and humorous man. The kind of man you could tell anything to, and he would have a similar story," Cara replied over the brothers' shouts and laughter.

"And his mother?"

Cara had been taking a sip of her wine and at the question almost snorted it up her nose with laughter. "She was one of a kind. She either loved you or hated you, and she left no confusion on which it was. She didn't like me too much at first."

Laurel was surprised by that; she hardly knew Cara, but she seemed like a sympathetic kind of person. "Why?"

She reached down and grabbed a slice of pizza, taking a bite and swallowing before she answered. "I'm sure David told you about Tim's health problems."

Laurel nodded.

"She wasn't about to relinquish her little boy to anyone who wouldn't be capable of taking care of him like she did. We almost broke up over it."

David had told her his mother was someone to reckon with. "She was that bad?"

"Yes and no. We were still young and in our first year of college. She just didn't think I could grasp the gravity of what he'd been through."

"David told me he was fine and had been for years before he went to college."

"That was the rub. He was fine, but she could never seem to let her guard down about that. It really ticked me off until I became a mother. We bonded over Drew because I was suddenly faced with a love I never understood before. If I had dealt with the same thing she had with Tim, I'd feel the same way. Once she realized I knew that, our whole relationship changed. I really miss that old pain in the neck."

Laurel laughed. "David told me she was quite opinionated but filled with total love."

Cara smiled. "I think that accurately sums her up."

****

Thanksgiving morning found David's house filled with laughter and chatter. Laurel had helped him dress the turkey the day before, and it was chilling in a roasting pan in the refrigerator. She had prepared side dishes to bake or warm up at her home and would bring them over to his house to finish cooking. He had asked her to spend the night, but she was old-fashioned enough to not think it proper with young children in the house. She had more cookware at her disposal at her house, and it made everything easier to prepare.

He gave her a call. "Cara is making breakfast for

us. Pancakes, sausages, fruit, muffins, you name it."

"You don't have to ask me twice."

She packed up her casserole dishes and headed for his house. She thought nothing smelled more enticing than a turkey roasting, but the spicy scent of sausages was equally tempting.

"You didn't have to do all this," Laurel told Cara.

"I love to cook, and it's the least I could do. You've done all the Thanksgiving cooking." She looked into the living room when she heard the men and kids laughing. "What are those idiots watching?"

Laurel checked the living room and told her with humor, "Educational programming. I think we generally refer to it as cartoons."

No sooner had they finished breakfast than the turkey had to start roasting. They had decided to eat later in the day allowing the children to play outside. It had snowed overnight; it was the wet, sticky kind that was conducive to making snowmen. It was unlikely the weather would stay cold enough for the snow to remain for very long, but it would keep the kids occupied and probably the brothers as well.

It didn't take the kids long to beg to get into the snow. Laurel rummaged through the refrigerator for a couple of carrot to be used as snowman noses and with the absence of coal she gave them grapes to use as a mouth and eyes. David dug through the hall closet and found some scarves and hats to add to their collection. Cara and Laurel remained in the warm house cooking and getting to know each other better. Periodically they would peer out the window to watch the snowmen progress.

Curiosity got the better of her. "Did you know

David's fiancée?"

When Cara didn't immediately answer, Laurel was afraid she may appear to be pumping her for information, but she answered seemingly without reserve. "We saw very little of her because we were in Boston, but yes I knew her."

"David told me a little bit about her and how it ended, but nothing of her personality."

In a direct response she said, "The total opposite of you."

Reluctantly, Laurel probed. "How so?"

"She liked to be noticed. She was the life of the party and overly flirtatious. From what I observed, she liked the idea of being a doctor's wife."

"David said she left him because she thought he worked too much."

Cara was disgusted at the thought of David's fiancée. "That was as good of an excuse as any; she got a better offer and took it."

"David is not foolish. How was he taken in?"

"All men are fools when pretty women fawn all over them. The things that attracted him to her were ultimately the things that drove them apart. She could be very endearing and fun, and David tended to be more serious. She could make him laugh like no one else and bring him back down again in an instant. It would never have worked, and he was lucky she left when she did, although he doubted that at the time."

Cara smiled. "I don't think he has those doubts any longer."

Chapter Seventeen

Laurel could not remember the last time she had such an enjoyable Thanksgiving. The playful banter between David and his brother, the energetic enthusiasm of the children, and girl talk with Cara made for a real holiday celebration.

Tim asked David, "I don't suppose the pond at Pioneer Cemetery is frozen over yet?"

He shook his head. "No, usually that doesn't happen until January."

"Too bad, it would have been nice to take the kids ice skating there like we used to as kids."

"People ice skate on the duck pond?" Laurel asked.

David seemed surprised by her ignorance. "You grew up here and never knew that?"

"Obviously, my education had been lacking."

Tim explained between bouts of laughter. "We had some great times there. The pond isn't deep, but the cemetery crew keeps it cordoned off until they test it for safety. No one is supposed to be on it unless an employee of the cemetery is present. They set hours for the community, and sometimes they had evening skating with lights. Naturally, David and I would sneak over to play hockey until we would get caught."

"I think my days of jogging are over until spring. It's too slippery and steep to run even when it's been plowed," David said. "I guess I'll have to resort to the gym, though it's not the same as being outside in the fresh air."

Cara suggested, "Maybe before we leave, we could put a wreath on your parents' grave."

There was sadness in Tim's voice when he said, "I haven't been there since Mom died."

"Until I started running, I had avoided it, too. I take solace in that it is a place for the living and brings so much peace and beauty to the residents. Did I tell you that's where I met Laurel?"

Cara's eyebrows lifted in a bemused expression. "In the cemetery?"

Laurel smiled. "Long story short, I was visiting my parents' grave, tripped over a tree root, and cracked my head open. He happened by on his run and patched me up. The rest is history."

"That will be a story for your kids," Tim said and then realized he was being presumptuous. "I'm sorry, just a figure of speech."

David's family stayed through Sunday, then headed back to Boston. They issued an open-ended invitation for them to visit any time. Laurel was excited about the prospect of showing David around a city where she had lived for several years. She, Tim, and Cara had endless conversations about all the places they had in common.

Winter had set in earlier than usual, much to the pleasure of the school-age children. Pioneer Cemetery Pond froze over, and the children were anxious to skate on it during their holiday break. The town parks department stepped in and relieved the cemetery association of the responsibility of safeguarding the community. The cemetery was already working with a tight budget, and it was an enormous help to their bottom line. It also allowed more ice time for the kids.

Laurel called Janet and asked if Missy and M.J. would like to go skating and then have hot chocolate at her house. Janet seemed to her a little reticent at first, but Missy had been doing well with no relapses. Laurel heard Mike yelling in the background, "We'll be there."

Laurel assured her friend she could take Missy to her house if her husband and son wanted to stay a little longer. The plan had been preapproved by David. Everyone knew he had grown up with a chronically ill brother and knew the importance of balancing fun with caution. Laurel could only image his mother's reaction when Tim wanted to do all the things the other kids did. David's presence put everyone at ease. It was exactly what was needed. Christmas was around the corner; the kids were off from school, and all were in a jovial mood.

Laurel's skating stills were modest, but David assured her the real secret was a well-fitted pair of skates. As a former high school and college hockey player, he could speed across the ice in an instant. She managed to stay upright but didn't expect the U.S. Olympic team contacting her any time soon.

Janet saw that Missy was tiring. "Can we go back to your place now? Mike and David can bring MJ with them later."

They had expected Missy to protest, but she had learned a lesson a child her age seldom did, how to pace herself. Once back at Laurel's, they stoked the fireplace, and while they were making cocoa, Missy fell sound asleep under a blanket in front of the fire. Janet looked lovingly upon her child and said, "You've been a really good friend."

"I could say the same of you. You never wavered in your support of me, and I didn't fully appreciate that at first. This last year has been a whirlwind of events. Sometimes it's a little scary not knowing what's next."

Janet looked at her sleeping daughter. "I know what you mean." She burst into tears.

Laurel instantly tried to comfort her. "Is there something I don't know?"

She shook her head. "No, I'm just emotional because I wasn't sure we'd have another Christmas with her."

Laurel put her arms around Janet. "You'll have many Christmases with her."

Janet leaned against Laurel's shoulder for support. "I believe that too; with all my heart."

Laurel's front door burst open, they heard the stomping of feet knocking snow off their boots and David calling, "Hot chocolate, hot chocolate."

Janet said, "Get those wet things off, and we'll warm you up."

While the women made more hot chocolate, MJ went over to where his sister was snuggled under a blanket near the fire and lay down next to her. She didn't even wake up through all the commotion. Laurel caught a glimpse of David watching them, and she knew exactly what he was thinking; it could have been him and his brother years earlier.

Mike said to Laurel and David, "This has been a much-needed respite. I feel like I am the luckiest man in the world. Maybe it's the hope of Christmas, maybe it's good friends, but either way I'm at peace."

An hour later, the Millers roused their children and

headed home. When the door closed behind them, Laurel tried conveying her emotions. "I can't express how I feel."

"Try," he encouraged as he drained the last of the hot chocolate into their mugs.

"Honestly, I was never unhappy, at least until this mess I've been dealing with this past year. I had a comfortable life, people who loved me, but…"

He stopped her. "Something was missing."

"Yes, did you feel it, too?"

"Not until Tim came with his family. It took me back to our childhood. I can be cavalier about it now that we're grown and he's all right, but even when we weren't certain he'd make it, there was a bond only a family can truly understand."

"I was an only child, but we had that, too. Sometimes money was tight, but having family made all the difference. I can't imagine not having family. It doesn't necessarily have to be our biological relatives, but that feeling is the same. Janet has become a sister to me in spirit."

David looked deep into her eyes. "Laurel, let's build on this. I know it hasn't yet been a year since your life, as you knew it, ended, but isn't this one better?"

She could not have agreed with him more. "It is. The past is the past, and it should stay there. We've each had our heartbreak and come out on the other side."

He smiled as he pulled her into his arms. "Let's bring in the new year with that purpose. I know we have all the elements to make a life together. We've learned from our mistakes. I'm not rushing you into anything."

"So, this is not a proposal?" she asked, not certain if she wanted it to be or not.

He leaned in for a kiss. "It's a proposal for a proposal."

"That works for me."

****

They spent a quiet Christmas together. The holiday did not slow David's practice down; kids were still getting sick or having accidents with daring sledding exploits. Laurel's office was quiet until after the first of the year. Everyone was on vacation until the first week in January. That did not stop her from exploring new and innovative ideas for the foundation.

One of the Christmas gifts David bought her was an expensive pair of ice skates. When she opened them, she said, "I think your money was wasted on these; I'll never skate as well as you."

"All the more reason for me to hold onto you. It may have been a bit self-serving on my part to buy them for you, but I like being out in the fresh air and I can't run right now."

She did not want him to think she was not appreciative. "I enjoy it, I really do. I'm just not a very good skater."

"I'll teach you. We will have to go early in the morning before the kids get out there so no one runs into you. The parks department has a sign out that the ice is safe, so they don't need to monitor it. If it warms up, they will close it, but I don't see that happening for a while. We can go there pretty much any time we want."

David had to make hospital rounds but told Laurel he would meet her at the pond at eight in the morning.

He finished early and was there before she arrived. It was cold but not windy nor currently snowing. The ice looked perfectly clear and smooth. He had seen hockey dads get together and occasionally shovel or sweep the ice to keep it as slick as possible. While sitting on a bench lacing up his skates, the woman who had helped him during his meltdown joined him.

In a friendly exchange, David asked, "What are you doing out in this chilly weather?"

"I know it's not the popular opinion, but winter is my favorite season. I find the snow and cold air exhilarating. I wanted to get out here before the children start skating."

He nodded. "That's why I'm here this early. Laurel will be joining me soon."

She grinned at him. "Laurel? Is that the woman you told me about?"

"It is. Your advice was flawless. I think she may be the one."

Nodding she said, "You could be right. Just remember no relationship comes without unexpected bumps in the road. Keep your eye on the larger picture, and you can get through anything."

"Thank you, I will."

"I'll let you get to your skating. I'm sure we'll run into each other again. Happy New Year, a few days early."

"Same to you," he replied, watching her as she navigated the snow-covered lanes. He thought about what she had said about unexpected bumps, and it was as if she knew something he did not. He realized it was a generalized statement, and certainly there was nothing more to it than that. While he was pondering that thought, he saw Laurel's car coming toward him.

She sat down next to him to lace up her skates. "I thought for sure I would beat you here and get a little practice in before you arrived."

"I only had one patient to check on, the other had been released. We try to release the kids in the hospital during the holidays, but sometimes it's necessary for them to stay." He extended his hand, pulling her to her feet. "Let's get you ready for the Olympics."

She was doing well and insisted upon navigating the ice alone. She had skated a little as a child, but she thought those days were behind her. She was enjoying the experience. "You were right about the value of a good pair of skates. My ankles are not wiggling at all."

Unfortunately, they had only skated for a half hour when a minivan pulled in and several children climbed out with hockey sticks. "That's our cue to leave," he said.

They were unlacing their skates when he said, "You barely missed that woman I was telling you about who walks here."

"Seriously? I wouldn't think she'd be out here today in this cold. I bet even Maggie wouldn't venture out."

"She said she loves the cold."

"I do too, but if you ask me that again at the end of February, my opinion may be different."

They drove into the village to have breakfast at the diner. There had been a sign up for a New Year's Eve celebration in the town square. It had been a hundred-year-old town tradition. "Would you like to go?" he asked.

She shook her head. "I don't think so. Chaz used to

drag me out every year to some sort of drunken party, and I never really enjoyed it."

"Did he? Enjoy them, I mean."

"Very much. He always liked lively events with lots of people and noise. He generally ended up drinking too much and saying things to people he probably shouldn't."

"I've gotten the impression from the little snippets you have told me about your marriage, that you did a lot of compromising."

She sighed as she thought about it. "I never gave it much consideration at the time, but I guess I did. I have never been a confrontational person; not that I didn't stand my ground, when necessary, but some things didn't matter."

Normally David avoided delving into her marital past, but they were now in a relationship, and it was important to be honest. He asked, "Would he have been as accommodating?"

She laughed at her own ignorance. "He had a way of making me think he would. I can see that now. No wonder he had been so successful at deceiving people, especially himself."

"You still don't hate him, do you?"

"What's the point of hating anyone? I don't want to bring any negativity into our relationship, and Chaz is certainly negative."

He changed the subject. "What would you like to do for New Year's?"

"If it's not too late to get reservations, I'd really love to dine at the Autumn Hill Inn."

"The owner seems to like you. I bet if you called and talked with him personally, he'd make room for us.

We've been regulars since our first date."

Laurel said, "I'll ask for something in the late afternoon, that way our last-minute reservation won't cut into any party celebrations he may have scheduled. Most people want late dining hours on New Year's Eve. They aren't old fogeys like us."

Laurel had been correct The Inn was able to accommodate them at six pm, seating them in the small informal dining room. It suited them perfectly, and they were not rushed through their meal. They enjoyed all the holiday decorations, which would remain for only a few more days. Laurel admired the twinkling lights and endless garlands.

"The worst thing about the holidays is taking down the decorations. For a few days, everything seems so lifeless and bare."

He laughed. "It will only be barren for five minutes because as soon as the Christmas and New Year's stuff is gone, there will be Valentine's Day hearts everywhere. Speaking of which, if you want to return here for that, we had better make reservations before we leave."

"I'd like that. Mr. Zander knows all the nuances of making the most of any holiday."

They lingered over their meal until they realized the place was beginning to fill up with diners. They were sensitive to the fact they had last minute reservations and did not want to take up valuable seating. David motioned to the waitress for the bill. She told them that it had already been paid and to have a Happy New Year.

"That was sweet of Mr. Zander not to charge us," Laurel said. "It wasn't necessary."

David placed a generous tip on the table. "He must have wanted to show his appreciation for our patronage. We do dine here regularly."

"If he did that for every frequent diner, he'd go broke. This is a popular date-night establishment. Whatever his reason for doing it, I'll send him a nice thank you note."

He helped her with her coat. "Your place or mine?"

"Pretty confident, aren't you?"

He took her hand, leading her to the car. "I'm not starting the New Year without you. If you make it as memorable as this one has been, I'll be a happy man."

"Why don't we stay at your place? I know you're on call again, and if you must leave, it would just make it easier for you to change. Drop me off at home so I can get my car and grab a few things, and I'll drive over to your house."

She went inside to put on something comfortable to wear, but she was suddenly hit with an odd, uneasy feeling. There was nothing wrong, everything was where it was supposed to be, and yet, it felt different. She shrugged it off, grabbed an overnight bag, and headed to David's house.

Once at his place, that feeling left her. He had made her a drink, put on soft music as they snuggled together waiting for the stroke of midnight, thus ending a both challenging and rewarding year.

Chapter Eighteen

Laurel was sound asleep with her head on David's chest when his phone rang. He reached over to grab it, waking her up. "It's my service," he said, then directed his conversation to the caller. "Tell them I'll meet them at my clinic in twenty minutes. It's not necessary for them to drive to the hospital."

As he slid out of bed and reached for his pants he said, "I'm sorry, honey, but I have to go."

"Is something wrong?"

"Not really wrong, more of an inconvenience for the family. One of the kids has a fever and severe sore throat. Two other members of the family have strep throat, and I'm certain that's the case with this one. I don't want to just assume that and order an antibiotic if that isn't what's going on, but I'm ninety-nine percent sure it is. I'll know quickly enough. You can stay in bed if you like."

She stretched and began to get out of bed. "I'm awake anyway. I'll take a quick shower and head home. Come by whenever."

As he was pulling on his sweatshirt, he looked out the window. "It started snowing again. It's been doing that off and on all night."

She laughed. "Well, it is winter."

After her shower, she gathered up her things and drove home. When she pulled up beside her paper box to get the holiday news edition, she noticed tire tracks going down and back out her driveway. She got out to investigate and saw large footprints, likely belonging to a man. The person apparently walked up to the front door and when no one answered tried to look in the front window. There was no evidence the person went beyond that point. She was not frightened, but she was certainly curious. She thought Janet's husband may have stopped by for some reason. She was always baking things and sending them over.

She gave Janet a call to ask, but she assured her they had not left the house. She shrugged off the incident; there were many reasons someone could have stopped by.

An hour later, her doorbell rang. She was certain David had forgotten the key she gave him. Laughing, she pulled open the door and started to say, "Since when do you..." The words trailed off.

It wasn't David standing at her door but Chaz.

She wasn't prone to such things, but she felt certain she was going to faint her shock was so great. She must have seemed unsteady because he reached out to take her arm.

"Are you all right?"

She stammered. "What—what—how—what are you doing here?"

"May I come in and explain?"

Words would not even pass her lips; she simply nodded. He came into the cottage, a place where he had spent many hours while his mother-in-law was still living, and sat on the sofa. She took a chair opposite him. She was still having difficulty catching her breath when she asked, "I thought you were in a country without extradition? They'll throw you in jail if they catch you. I can assure you I won't cover for you."

"No, they won't. I've paid my debt to society."

With both anger and disgust, she raised her voice. "I'm not likely to believe that. You defrauded me and your clients out of millions. You were facing years in prison. There is no way the FBI isn't looking for you."

He was perfectly calm and remained reasonable. He seemed in all manner the same Chaz she once thought she knew. "My presence here is perfectly legal."

Shaking her head, she said, "That's not possible."

"There was someone the FBI wanted more than me, and I had the means to deliver him. I was cut a deal to plead guilty to a couple of felonies, accept probation with no jail time."

"They can do that?"

"I'm not a violent criminal, even you would have to admit that."

He was right about that; she knew he would never physically harm anyone, but she still was not satisfied, and his story seemed preposterous. "Nonetheless, you destroyed many lives. That doesn't matter?"

He hung his head in what appeared to be genuine remorse. "It does matter, and I'm truly sorry for it, more for you than the others. I betrayed the one person who meant the world to me."

She tried not to cry, but the tears came anyway. "You ripped my heart out, destroyed my reputation, and left me close to broke. If my mother hadn't left me this house, I'd have been homeless."

"A woman with a Harvard MBA was highly unlikely to be homeless or broke for very long. I knew you'd pull yourself back up."

Anger spewed from her lips. "So that made it all right."

"Of course not, I'm not trying to justify any of my actions, just explain them."

She got up and paced the floor, looking back over her shoulder at him, not entirely believing he was there. He continued, "If you could forgive me, I'm willing to forgive you."

She could only stare at him. "Just what are you forgiving me for?"

He did not seem particularly upset. "It looks like you wasted no time in replacing me."

"We're divorced. Do you want a copy of the decree?"

"I've seen you with the good doctor."

"Just how long have you been in town? Have you been following us?" She was terrified by that prospect.

"Long enough to buy your dinner last night. I see you're still a fan of Mr. Zander's cuisine."

Her eyes grew large. "That was you? I thought Mr. Zander was our benefactor."

He stood up to take a few steps toward her, as she backed up just as quickly to get away from him. "I'm not blaming you. You were alone and needed someone. I haven't been a monk either, but I never stopped wanting to be with you. We can start over with a clean slate."

"You can't be serious. Did you think I'd open my arms to welcome you back? You're delusional."

"I'm getting back on my feet. My brother has a small manufacturing company in California. I'm managing the financial end of it for him."

The idea was so absurd, she laughed. "Is he out of his mind? You'll cheat him out of every dollar he has."

He sounded almost offended she would suggest such a thing. "I wouldn't do that."

She was waving her hands with rage. "You can hardly expect me to believe that. I loved you and you ruined me, or at least you nearly did."

He was the only one remaining calm as he explained, "It was never my intention to ruin anyone. I got in over my head. Whether you knew it or not, that had happened to me half a dozen times, and I always managed to pull things together. This last time I had too many things stacked against me. If I didn't want to go to jail, I knew I had to leave."

She suspected he was telling the truth about that part; even her attorney had suggested as much. "You didn't have to leave. You could have been a man and faced the consequences."

He shrugged. "I could have, but who would that have helped? My clients would still be out the money, and my leaving saved you from a worse fate. You would have stood by me, even when I went to jail. You can't help yourself, you're that kind of person. This way you were a victim too and would be treated with sympathy."

Her mouth literally hung open from disbelief. When she found her voice, she said, "So, you thought you were doing me a favor—thank you so much."

"Don't be sarcastic, Laurel. It was better this way."

"Better," she repeated quietly. "Do you know what better was? I was fired from my job. The FBI thought you may have had my cooperation in manipulating bank funds. I had reporters at my door with cameras and microphones stuck in my face. My bank accounts were frozen, and yes, I lost our house. You forged my signature, and they foreclosed on me. I had no home, no money, and no credit."

He made a sweeping gesture for the cottage. "You had this."

"I wouldn't even have had this if you had your way. You kept trying to talk me into selling it. If my own grief hadn't caused me to procrastinate on probating my mother's will, it would have been taken from me, too."

"But it wasn't, and you landed another job. You seem to be doing all right."

It took every ounce of reserve she possessed to keep from lunging at him. "You left me with nothing but my self-respect, and even that was shaken. Fortunately for me, there were people willing to give me a chance. I haven't, nor won't, give them any reason to second-guess their trust."

"See," he began, "that's exactly why I need you. You are my moral compass."

Her body dropped back down in a chair from sheer exhaustion. "Apparently, I have been demagnetized. It's useless and so are you. I want you to leave and never contact me again."

"I know all this has been a shock to you, and you need time to process it. I'm staying at the motor lodge outside of Bridgefield. I'll give you a few days to think things over. I've got a modest apartment in northern California near my brother's factory. We could live there together until you found another job."

Laurel stood, went to the front door, and screamed at the top of her lungs, "Get out."

"I'll give you some time to reconsider."

He got back in his rental car and drove off. She became physically ill. Her entire body was shaking. She pulled a quilt around her and curled up into a catatonic ball on the sofa. She was so distraught she never heard any of David's text messages telling her he was bringing home a pizza. A couple of hours later he arrived, completely oblivious to anything that had happened.

As he carried the pizza toward the kitchen, he caught a glimpse of the back of her head as she huddled on the sofa. He started jabbering about his day as he pulled plates from the kitchen cabinets for the pizza slices. "I was right; it was strep throat. Before I could leave two more cases came in." He didn't wait for a comment. "I could really use a glass of wine. Do you want one or would you prefer ice water?"

She still did not answer. He took a few steps toward the living room. "Laurel, did you hear me?"

Still there was only silence, which worried him as he approached her. All he saw was her tear-streaked face staring blankly at nothing. He got down on his knees next to the sofa and gently shook her. "My God, Laurel, what's wrong?"

She could only whisper. "He was here."

He jumped to his feet in a panic and looked around the room thinking someone had attacked her. "He? Who is he? Are you hurt?"

She just shook her head in the negative and pulled the quilt tighter around herself.

"Laurel, please, I need more information, you're scaring me."

"Chaz."

"Your ex-husband, Chaz? What did he want? How did he get here? I'm calling the police," he said and reached for his phone.

She finally spoke more than a single word. "There's no point in calling the police. He's not wanted for anything."

She started crying, so he pulled her into his arms to comfort her, but he still didn't know anything. It seemed more important to hold her than drag answers from her. Laurel was a sensitive person but not an emotional one, and she was frightening him.

After what seemed like an eternity, he was able to get her to talk. She wiped her face with the edge of the quilt and apologized. "I'm sorry for acting this way. I was more blindsided by his reappearance than I was his disappearance."

"I can understand that, but what I don't understand is why he is not in jail."

"Apparently he had valuable information on someone that allowed him to cut some kind of a deal."

"I know that happens all the time, but it doesn't seem fair that he could ruin people's lives and run around a free man. Maybe he is lying to you. It's not like he's known for being an honest man."

"He must have been here for a while because he knew about you, about us."

"He's been following us?"

"He was the one who paid for our dinner at the Inn."

"What does he want?"

"Me."

"Did he actually think you would say, 'All's forgiven, let's start over'?"

"That's exactly what he thought. He was even going to be so gracious as to forgive me for being with you."

David had reason to be concerned for her safety. The mere fact he had been stalking them proved he was unstable or maybe even delusional. "Did he threaten you in any way?"

She was slowly becoming more composed. "Not at all, in fact, he was the same old Chaz. He was calm and confident I'd pick up where we left off."

"I'm suddenly developing an insight into the real Chaz Tanner. He has a narcissistic personality disorder. Fortunately, he has not been violent or threatening in any manner. If he wants something, he thinks he's entitled to it at any cost. The fact that others may be hurt is irrelevant. You lived with it for so long you never saw him for what he was; especially because he had a seemingly affable personality. What did you tell him?"

She looked shocked that he would even ask. "I threw him out of here and told him to never contact me again."

David took a deep breath, exhaled, and said in a slow deliberate voice, "That won't be good enough. Someone like Chaz will keep coming back until or unless he can be made to understand he has more to lose than gain."

"I made it clear I didn't want to see him. He has no power over me any longer."

"I'm not so certain of that."

"You can't possibly think I'd choose him over you."

"There was a time I may have thought that, but not

now. We're past those kinds of insecurities."

"Then what are you talking about?"

"Laurel look at yourself, your reaction. He was able to get to you. That's exactly what he was hoping to do. He needs you, but you certainly don't need him. We've all made mistakes in our past, chose the wrong person, and sometimes even try to justify it in our own minds. I know you don't want to think he is irredeemable because then you'd have to admit you wasted a lot of years with him in your marriage. He senses your vulnerability and knows your kind heart. Let it go."

She wiped her runny nose on the quilt still wrapped around her. "I will once I know he's gone."

"He's not going to leave just because you told him to go. He hasn't come all this way not to get what he wants. Do you know where he is?"

"He said he was staying at the motor lodge outside of Bridgefield. He's hoping I will change my mind."

There was agitation in his voice. "Do you see my point?"

"When I don't show up, I think it should be obvious I want nothing to do with him."

David raised his voice. "Come on, Laurel, get your head out of the sand. You said he's been stalking us; do you honestly think he's going to give up this easily?"

"I could get a restraining order. If it's true he's on probation, the authorities won't like that. Perhaps the threat of going to prison if he's in violation might be a motivating factor in staying away. It was the prospect of going to prison that made him run away in the first place."

"It's been my experience a restraining order isn't

worth the paper it's written on. Chaz is the type of man who would be looking for the loophole. His recent reprieve is evidence enough of that. It would be a joke to him."

Laurel asked helplessly, "If not that, what?"

David got up and went for his coat before answering. "I'm going to kick his ass."

She scrambled to her feet and stood between him and door. "Don't go there. We must stand firm until he knows there is no pathway back to me. Eventually he'll return to California where he has been living. We'll wait him out."

David pulled her away from the door. "I'm not willing to take that chance. He's leaving tonight."

"David, don't go, he's not worth it."

"You're right. He's not. But you are."

Chapter Nineteen

David was getting into his car when Laurel ran out of the house. She did not even take the time to put on a coat but leapt into the passenger's seat before he could object. His lips were pursed so tightly they were turning purple. "You're not going with me."

She was undeterred. "If you go, I go."

Neither uttered a word the entire drive to the motor lodge. After pulling up in front of the office, they went inside. "Where can we find Charles Tanner's room?" David asked.

"He must be a popular man," the elderly attendant said. He then extended his hand clearly indicating he wanted a bribe. David slapped a twenty-dollar bill in it. "You'll find him in room eleven."

Laurel only briefly wondered what the man meant by that, but they soon found out. They drove around to the room and saw Chaz's door open to the cold afternoon air. They heard an angry exchange of words but could not make them out. David took the lead, with Laurel right behind him, as they pushed the door open to a terrifying scene.

Chaz faced them, a look of horror on his face, as a man held him at gunpoint. Chaz yelled, "He's going to kill me."

When the man turned, David uttered, "Durant?"

"Get out of here, both of you. This is between me

and this worthless piece of trash," he said in a remarkably calm voice.

"He's been thinking about this," David whispered to Laurel. "Otherwise, he would be as nervous as Chaz."

In a sympathetic tone Laurel tried to be the voice of reason. "Mr. Durant, please don't do this."

"I would think, you of all people, would enjoy watching him die."

The smile on Durant's face indicated he was reveling in Chaz's desperation. He added to it by releasing the cylinder on the revolver so it would pop open. Then, for effect, snapping it shut with enough force the sound made Chaz jump. Durant laughed and cocked the gun.

Suddenly David's demeanor changed. "You must admit," he told her, "the man's got a point."

"David!" Laurel exclaimed.

"Think about it for a minute. If Chaz is dead, all our problems are solved. He won't bother us again and Mr. Durant would have gotten his revenge. I'd call that a mutually beneficial outcome."

"Laurel, do something," Chaz said, his voice quivering.

"Are you two out of your mind?" Laurel yelped. "Mr. Durant, you'll go to prison for the rest of your life. David, for God's sake, you're a doctor."

"I'll even sign the death certificate," he offered.

Durant never took his eyes off Chaz, nor did he loosen his grip on the revolver. "And I'm an old man, how many more years do I have? A good lawyer could stall a trial for years, or better yet, cut me a sweetheart deal like ole Chaz here got."

Laurel argued for reason. "We're still talking about a human life."

David shrugged. "Are we really?"

She stared at him in disbelief. This is not the man she had fallen in love with, the man with whom she'd considered spending the rest of her life.

In a high-pitched squeak, Chaz said, "I'll go away. You'll never see me again. I promise I won't tell anyone about this."

Durant glanced briefly at David who stood behind at his shoulder. "Do you think I can believe him?"

"I've never met him before, so I can't say." David then looked at Laurel. "You know him best. Will he keep his word? He did come back here once after he ran away like a coward."

"Laurel," Chaz shouted. "Tell them I'll leave. I won't ever bother any of you again."

She looked at Mr. Durant. "For all our sakes, you'll have to let him go."

In a cold impersonal voice, Durant replied, "You've got three minutes to get out of here, or I'll pull the trigger."

In record time, Chaz jammed everything he had into his suitcase, all while Mr. Durant's gun remained trained on him. As Chaz ran for the door he hesitated, only briefly, in front of Laurel. He looked like wanted to say something, but the next sound they heard was the slam of a car door and tires spinning out of the snowy parking lot.

David and Durant burst into hysterical laughter, while Laurel stared at them as if they had gone insane. "How'd you know I wasn't going to shoot him?" Durant asked David.

Still laughing David said, "I didn't at first. It wasn't until you popped open the cylinder that I could see you didn't have a bullet in it. No one who was intent on killing someone would not have a fully loaded gun."

Laurel was not entirely certain whether she was relieved or angry. This, even after everything she had been through, was the worst experience she ever had. She was certain Mr. Durant was going to kill Chaz; the police would investigate, and scandal would haunt her and David for the rest of their lives.

"How did you even know he was here?" she asked.

"I've had a private investigator on the case since it first happened. I was determined Chaz Tanner was going to prison. He was the type of man who would screw up eventually. I was even prepared to have someone trick him into entering a country where he could be extradited. What I hadn't predicted was the opportunity he had to turn state's evidence. That put him beyond my reach, but I sure as hell could keep him away from here. I'll never forgive or forget how he hurt the people who trusted me."

"I'm going to find out who his probation officer is and where they are located," David said. "I'm certain they can make it a condition of his continued probation he never contact Laurel again."

Mr. Durant said, "I don't want one more person to be cheated by him, so I'm going to the motel office and making sure his bill is paid. It will be money well spent. I hope you two have a very happy New Year."

Laurel was shivering when they got back inside David's car. He took off his coat and gave it to her and turned the heat up in the car to its maximum. The drive home had been as silent as the one to the motor lodge only for different reasons. She was clearly shaken to her core.

Once safely back in her house he asked, "Aren't you going to say anything?"

"How could you have let that happen to me?" she demanded.

"Laurel be reasonable, I was hardly in a position to explain what Durant was doing. It was sheer providence that I caught on. It's over, we're through with Chaz."

"I want to believe that, but are things going to continue to resurface? I don't mind for myself; I must accept my part. You, on the other hand, are a complete innocent. In one simple act of anger, you could have destroyed your career. What would you have done if Mr. Durant hadn't gotten there first?"

He shook his head. "I'm not entirely certain what I would have done. If you hadn't jumped in my car to go along, it would have been worse than if you weren't there. It would have depended on his actions, I suppose."

"He was never physically confrontational and would have told you what you wanted to hear to get rid of you and then do what he wanted. That's the way he has always been."

"I'm certain that Durant knew that, too, and it was his reason for taking extreme measures. I don't think I would have gone that far, but I applaud his imagination."

Laurel did not share his opinion. Everything seemed to have worked out, but the possibility that it could have gone horribly wrong tormented her.

"What are you thinking?" David asked. "I need to

know what's going on in your head."

"I don't want to lose this, but how many relationships are tested in such a dramatic display?"

"Laurel, it's important to me for you to realize I'd protect you at all costs; I love you. No one is guaranteed an easy ride, but the trip will be worth it, I promise you that." He reached out to her for an embrace.

She looked so sad. "I feel the same way about you, which is why you should rethink being with me. I'm damaged goods. No matter how hard I try I can't seem to escape the mistakes I've made."

"We've danced around this issue before; you are not responsible for anything Chaz has done. I'd like to say he has to live with his mistakes, but somehow, I just don't think he is capable of any real remorse. The best we can hope for is karma to step in. It has with you."

She sounded disgusted. "That's what I'm afraid of. It's telling me to do better or pay the consequences."

"There's bad karma and good karma. Yours has been good and will continue to stay that way. A lot that is positive has come out of this. You have a job where you can really make a difference in people's lives, and you're appreciated for it. You're surrounded by the comfort and good memories of this house, and we have found each other. Why would you want to dwell on the negative? I honestly believe together we can tackle just about anything." He laughed nervously, adding, "The new year got off to a rocky start, but even good came of that."

"Escape while you can. Honestly, I won't hold it against you." She was sincere but also confused and weary.

"Exactly what is your worst fear? Is it that Chaz will never leave you alone?"

She couldn't help but crack a smile. "I'm certain Mr. Durant took care of that problem. Chaz is a coward at heart."

"If not that; what?"

"What if I'm just one of those people where things aren't meant to go right?"

"Now you're just feeling sorry for yourself. Besides the mess Chaz dragged you into, what in your life had been unsuccessful? You were a small-town girl from modest means, and yet you made it to Harvard. It opened doors and opportunities your parents could never have imagined possible for themselves but wanted for you. You didn't disappoint them or yourself."

"I want to believe that, but I'm almost afraid to."

She buried her head in sofa cushion to avoid looking at him, nevertheless she could feel the intensity of his stare. He sat next to her and gently rubbed her back. His touch was warm and comforting, but she was still unable to look him in the face. She could hear him fumbling for his phone; it didn't ring so she assumed it was on vibrate.

"The drug store is closed, but I have some samples at my clinic. Meet me there, and I'll give them to you." He returned to her. "I'm sorry, but I have to leave. I'll be back shortly."

She simply nodded in acknowledgement. He left, driving directly to the Miller's house. He rang the doorbell and Mike answered. "Good to see you, come on in."

Janet came into the hallway to see who had arrived.

"Is something wrong with Laurel? Do those footprints in the snow she called about have anything to do with you being here?"

He nodded, and she led him into the living room where they could talk. The kids had been playing nearby with their Christmas toys, so she asked them to take them into the family room.

"Do you need to talk?" she asked.

He was going to tell her about Chaz, but he had to think about what he would say. He did not want to mention Mr. Durant. It wasn't relevant to why he had come to see them. He carefully omitted his involvement.

"The tire tracks and footprints belonged to Chaz," he informed her.

"He had the nerve to come back here?" Janet asked. "Did she call the police?"

"She was going to, but he told her he made a deal with the government, and he was no longer a wanted felon."

"Do you believe that?" Mike asked.

"I haven't officially confirmed it, but I have every reason to believe it's true. That's not the point of why I'm here, at least not directly. I had words with him, which I won't detail, but he knows it is in his best interest to go away and never bother her again."

"Why are you here?" Janet asked.

"I know the two of you socialized as a couple and that you were friends with Chaz."

Mike interjected. "Friends would be a loose term; Janet and Laurel were friends; Chaz and I were *friendly*."

"I get what you're trying to say. You had no

objections to him, but he wasn't someone you'd take golfing."

Mike nodded. "Don't get me wrong. I did like the guy, but he was full of bull."

Janet added, "Laurel never said anything one way or another, but I could tell he often embarrassed her with his bragging. We tolerated him because we cared about her."

David said, "I thought it was something like that."

Janet looked at him intently and asked, "You aren't here just to ask about their life together, are you?"

He shook his head. "No. She's having a meltdown over this entire thing and questioning her self-worth."

"I couldn't disagree with that more; however, I can see it from her point of view. We all tend to take responsibility for the actions of the people closest to us. As a mother, I know I do that. If they misbehave in public, you think everyone is judging you. That is an over-simplification of what she is feeling, but the principle is the same."

David looked relieved. "Then you get what I'm worried about?"

"Of course," Janet said. "What can I do?"

"Can you just go speak with her?" David asked. "She has told me many times that she thinks of you as a sister. She'll tell you things she wouldn't be comfortable telling me."

"You don't even have to ask me twice. She has been at my side every time I needed her during Missy's treatments. Is she at home?"

He nodded. "I'll drive you."

Mike grabbed his arm. "No, stay out of it. You're a good man and I trust you with our children's lives, but you need to back off. Let Janet talk to her."

David was silent as he watched Janet put on her coat. She went over to him and gave him a hug. "It'll be all right. This was all so sudden she hasn't had a chance to process it. She just needs to sort through a few things. I'll help her any way I can."

After Janet closed the door, Mike said, "You need a drink."

David replied, "I hope I wasn't out of line dragging the two of you into this, but I didn't know what else to do."

Mike patted him on the shoulder. "You did the right thing. If anyone can reason with her, it's my wife. They have been friends for a few years, but ever since Missy became ill, their friendship has deepened. She would consider it a partial payment for that friendship."

Janet drove directly to Laurel's house and pulled into the driveway. She caught a glimpse of her through the window and saw her huddled in a fetal position on the sofa. She rang the doorbell, and when she answered, they embraced. It was a similar exchange to the one they shared when Laurel had heard about Missy. Friends could read each other's emotions without spoken words, and Laurel needed that.

Chapter Twenty

"You've seen David, haven't you?" Laurel asked.

Janet nodded. "He's at my house with Mike."

She sighed. "I wish he hadn't bothered you. This is my mess."

There was compassion in Janet's voice when she said, "It's no bother, and please don't be angry. He loves you with all his heart."

Laurel was clearly depressed but resigned to the need to leave town. "I love him, too, which is why I'm going to call Tom Underwood and ask if that position in New York is still available."

"Are you out of your mind? What's wrong with you?"

"I think it's best for everyone. In New York, I will be just another anonymous worker drone. I certainly would never have to worry about running into Chaz. No reputable institutions would give him a second look. I'm good at what I do, and I can lose myself in my work and David can find someone with no baggage."

Janet could barely believe what she was hearing. "When have you ever met anyone without baggage? I have it, you have it, and David has it. There is nothing in that baggage you need, so unpack it. You do yourself and him a disservice if you run away."

"I can't quite explain it, but I can't shake an uneasy feeling."

"Did you feel it yesterday?" Janet asked.

"No, of course not, but Chaz hadn't shown up yet. At least, I didn't know about it."

"Doesn't that tell you something? You were happy and looking forward to the future with David. The corporate offices wanted you back, so you know they had moved past your circumstances. Why haven't you? Don't make me slap you."

Laurel gave a slight laugh. "How can I get myself back on track?"

Janet took her hands, looked her in the eye and replied. "The same way you did before—one day at a time. We've been friends for a few years now, and I've seen a big change in you."

Laurel did not feel any different. "How so?"

"You were always over-shadowed by Chaz. I'm not referring to the quality of your work; you were the best bank president the bank had ever known. You were organized, dependable, and compassionate, but you were content staying in the background. I saw other people get credit you deserved, but you let them take it. Chaz depended on that and thrived because of it. Isn't that what is really having you rattled?"

"I inadvertently empowered him."

"I'd have to agree with that; however, the operative word is, *inadvertently*. You can't go backward, and you don't want to. There is no place for you there. You started to shine once Chaz was gone and became your own person. Don't second-guess that person now. In just a year, you have made an impact for good in the community. Imagine what you could in—let's say five years—accomplish. If you are going to cheat yourself, you cheat all of us. If your heart gets broken this time, it will be of your own doing. Just remember you take David with you, and he's been the best thing that has ever happened to you."

Laurel was silent for a few seconds. "Would you mind asking David to give me some time to think things over? If I call him, he will want to see me and try to influence me. If I'm to get my head on straight, it must be of my own accord."

"I can do that, but only if you promise me, you won't leave him hanging. Take a day if you need it, but he needs transparency, and he's earned it."

****

The next morning David awoke to an awful headache. He had a vague memory of doing shots of whiskey with Mike. It was something he now deeply regretted, especially when he heard head-pounding clanging of pots from the kitchen. He wandered in to find Janet making breakfast for the children.

"How are you feeling?"

He drew his hands threw his hair. "Do I look awful?"

"Yep."

"Good, then I look how I feel."

Janet looked over at the kids. "Why don't you take your cereal into the family room and watch cartoons."

David heard them yell, "Yeah," as they disappeared.

"Would you like me to make you something to eat?

"God, no! How's Laurel?"

"We talked."

He heard the hangover-induced edge in his voice. "I figured that much. What did she tell you?"

Janet handed him a cup of coffee. "Without

divulging any confidences, I have hopes she will reconcile the contradictions she is feeling. She asked me to request you give her some time to think."

He took a sip of the hot beverage, then waited a minute to see if it would stay down before speaking. "How much time?"

"A day or two should do it."

He put the coffee cup on the counter. "Thank you, I know I was imposing on you. I think I'll go home now and vomit."

He grabbed his coat and headed for the door as Janet called out, "David, remember a day or two."

He simply nodded.

****

Laurel vacillated between staying and going back to New York. Her heart was here, but the appeal of impersonalizing her life was in New York. She had hoped the morning would have brought her clarity, but it hadn't. The rising sun was shining like diamonds on the freshly fallen snow. It was cold, but the lack of wind made for a pleasant day. She decided to go to the one spot which always offered her peace and perspective—Pioneer Cemetery. The pond should be free of children playing and quiet because school had resumed.

She bundled up, made a thermos of coffee, and drove to the pond. She spotted a couple of people in the distance cross-countryskiing down the lanes. It was a perfect environment for that. She was surprised it had never occurred to David to replace his jogging. She saw two people bundled in parkas with the hoods pulled securely over their heads. One of them waved to her as the other walked off. She waved back, knowing it would be Maggie. The old woman made her way to the bench and sat. "Happy New Year."

Laurel smiled. "Same to you. I didn't think you walked in this weather. I've been here several times ice skating, and I haven't seen you."

"I'm not a huge fan of the cold and snow."

"Then why are you out here?"

She pointed toward the person walking away. "My friend loves it, so occasionally I acquiesce. I do not share her love of the brisk winter air. I'm waiting for spring, and it can't come soon enough."

Laurel laughed. "You must be a good friend."

She smiled. "Friendships, like marriages, are about compromise."

Laurel wanted to take advantage of her wisdom. "How do you know how much to compromise?"

"When you feel like you are sacrificing your soul. No relationship is ever worth having if you can't be content with yourself first. No one has the right to expect an unequal exchange."

Still filled with despair, Laurel continued to seek answers. "What if you believe you may do more harm than good to someone you love?"

"Has that young doctor done something to you?"

Laurel quickly jumped to David's defense. "Oh no, he's perfect, too perfect for me."

Maggie laughed out loud. "No man is ever too perfect for a woman."

Despite herself, Laurel smiled. "Your husband must have his hands full with you."

"I like to think I keep him humble." Then she asked, "If he's so perfect, then what's the problem?"

Laurel sounded almost pathetic with her response.

"Me, it's always been me."

Maggie stared at her. "Does this have anything to do with your problem when I saw you here a few weeks ago?"

"It's all interrelated."

"Then your solution is the same."

"Listen to my heart and then my head?" Laurel asked, to recap their earlier conversation.

"Precisely. If this doctor is as perfect as you say he is, why would you throw away a chance on love? Trust me, it doesn't come along every day. You seem to be more concerned about your own failings; that's a good thing."

"In what way?"

"None of us are without them. The real blessing is to realize that and avoid them. It's the people that can't grasp that who end up ruining their lives. You're too smart for that. I suspect you have been presented with lessons to be learned and now you have."

"You make it sound simple."

Waving her hand in dismissal, Maggie laughed. "Nothing in life is simple, and if it were, it wouldn't be worth living. If this doctor is everything you think he is, don't deny him or yourself of a future. The past can't hurt you unless you let it." It started to snow again. Maggie looked up at the sky. "I think I had better get going while I can. I know a storm cloud when I see one."

Laurel was concerned for her elderly friend. "I'll give you a ride. I don't want you to fall."

"I can walk back quicker than you could drive me. Stay a little longer and think about what we discussed. Just don't let yourself freeze to the bench."

"Thank you, I've come to rely on your insight more than you'll ever know."

Maggie laughed. "It's nice to be good for something."

Laurel watched her as she cut across the cemetery and realized it was closer for her to walk home. She disappeared over a hill toward the development. Meanwhile she poured herself a hot cup of coffee from the thermos as she stared out onto the frozen pond. She smiled as she thought about ice skating with David. Everything seemed effortless when she was with him. She would hurt herself more than him if she went back to New York City. They complemented one another, and she realized there was nothing she would not do for him. If the roles had been reversed, she would have admonished him for disparaging himself. Why should she be more critical of herself?

As she pondered that thought, she heard a car drive up. She turned to see David get out and walk toward her. He sat next to her on the bench. "Janet told me you needed a little solitude to think. I promise you I wasn't stalking you. I was doing the same thing."

She smiled because she was genuinely happy to see him. "This does seem to be our go-to place to reflect."

"Maybe this is the wrong time and place, but I have something I want you to have. It's something I've been carrying around for a month." He reached into his interior coat pocket and took out a ring. It wasn't in a fancy velvet box, just the ring itself.

"It's beautiful."

"It was my mother's engagement ring. As the eldest son, she left it to me with a note that said, 'When you find the woman you want to spend the rest of your life with, put it on her finger and don't let her get away.' It's modest by today's standards, but I had it reset and added some accent diamonds. It's a little of the past and present and hopefully a long future."

She tried to hold back tears. "I have something for you, too," she said. "Me."

He helped her remove her left glove and then slipped the ring on her finger before they exchanged a passionate kiss.

"I should have known my ex-fiancée was not the right person because it never even occurred to me to give it to her. She wouldn't have appreciated the symbolism of it, and she wanted something big and flashy."

Laurel gazed at the sparkling diamonds with admiration. "It's perfect. I can almost feel your mother through it."

He laughed lightly. "I think I did things a bit backward and never said the words; Laurel, will you be my wife?"

A tear dripped down her cheek. "It would be my honor."

Chapter Twenty-One

To the delight of their close friends and David's brother, they began to make wedding plans. It was decided a spring wedding suited them best. The weather would be pleasant, and the blossoms and early perennials would be in full bloom. It also gave them time to plan their living arrangements.

David said, "I know how fond you are of your cottage, and you'd probably prefer to live there."

"I would, but you have a bigger house, and who knows, hopefully we'll need it."

"My house is just a house with no special attachment for me. You have a history and love for yours. There's plenty of room to expand if we need it."

She felt he was reading her mind. "That would mean a lot to me."

"I guess you could call this our first compromise."

Thinking about Maggie's words she said, "I'm certain it won't be our last."

David's brother happily agreed to be his best man and Janet, who was the closest person Laurel had to a sister, stood as matron of honor. Missy was assigned the duties of flower girl with her brother MJ being the ring bearer. David had discussed with his brother the possibility of his nephew assuming the duties, but everyone thought Missy's brother was the better choice.

The reception was to be held at Autumn Hill Inn,

but the choice of wedding venue took a few people aback. They wanted to be married at the pond in Pioneer Cemetery. The idea was fully embraced after they explained their choice. The cemetery was the place they met, sought comfort, and enjoyed community activities. Their request was not the first. Many marriages and wedding photo ops had included the historically scenic cemetery. Laurel was assured by the caretaker the swans would have returned and the flowering trees would be in full bloom by their wedding date.

The couple's choice to be married there had another significance; it was where generations of their family were in their final resting place. It was a way, in spirit, to include them.

Days before the wedding the couple decided to go through all their old family photos and create a montage of their families through the years. It was yet another way to include those who had gone before them. David brought over boxes of old photos and albums to select from, and Laurel did the same. Her dining room table was a history lesson of both their families. There was a lot of giggling and awing as they picked through the old pictures. They each started setting aside the ones they thought were significant.

After hours of flipping through photos, David stood up and stretched. "I need a glass of wine. Do you want one?"

"I won't say no," she replied as she continued the arduous task of selecting photos.

She pulled out a photograph marked *Heart Fund Appreciation Dinner*. She instantly recognized her mother in the center of the photo holding one half of a gigantic heart surrounded by two dozen other volunteers. It made Laurel smile because her mother looked just as she would always remember her.

David came up behind her to reach over and handed her the glass of wine. He looked at the picture and said, "I don't recall ever seeing that picture before, Mom looks great."

"Mom? This is of my mother."

"No, it isn't." He pointed to the woman holding the other side of the heart. "That's my mom."

Because the photo had been among Laurel's things, she never looked beyond her mother. She realized their mothers must have known each other. It wasn't until she took a closer look at David's mother and gasped. "That's your mother? That's Maggie."

"You mean the woman from the cemetery? That's not possible, they must have similar features."

He then dug through his box of photos and started laughing. "Okay, this is my mom, wearing her favorite outfit. She wanted to be buried in it."

He handed Laurel the picture and she turned pale as she looked at an elderly woman wearing a pink bathrobe and fuzzy pink slippers.

"Do you remember when you told me about the woman who helped you and I thought it was Maggie and you asked me what she was like? I told you I had seen her dressed that way, and you laughed and assured me the woman you knew was nothing like that."

"You can't be serious. My mother's name was Margaret. The only person who ever called her—" He stopped in mid-sentence, then continued, "—Maggie was my father."

"I'm almost afraid to ask, but take a good look at

the other person holding the heart. Is that your friend?"

He dropped heavily onto a dining room chair staring at the picture. He could not speak; he could only nod in the affirmative. He and Laurel continued to show each other pictures of their mothers, and neither had any doubt they were the same women.

"Is this even possible, or are we both crazy?"

"Maybe both. I don't think I even want to question it. I always said my mother would move Heaven and Earth for me; I guess she did. Admit it, deep down we both must have realized these women were our spiritual guides. I know every time I went to the cemetery, I hoped I'd see Maggie. I came to rely on her judgment and kindness."

Clutching a picture of Caroline, he said, "I just thought she was a nice lady who simply wanted to help. When I think about it the few times our paths crossed, she left me with a sense of serenity. It never occurred to me to doubt any of her advice."

****

Their wedding day arrived and, as they gathered with their friends and family, two extra guests stood atop a hill, watching their children exchange their vows.

"I wasn't so sure we'd pull this off," Maggie told Caroline.

"Oh, Margaret, ye of little faith."

The minister pronounced Laurel and David husband and wife. Before they kissed, David whispered, "Do you think they're watching?"

"I'm certain of it."

Their mothers each blew them a kiss as they faded into eternity.

A word about the author…

Writing is a second act for C. Ellen Culverwell; her first was law enforcement. After earning a degree in criminal justice, she was hired as the youngest and among the first women to be a Niagara County deputy sheriff. After leaving the force to raise her daughter, she continued to consult with various law enforcement agencies in matters of electronic surveillance. After the death of her husband, she turned to her passion for writing. Originally, her writing was meant to be cathartic, a means to empower her imagination. Her mantra has become, "Personal tragedy is only tragic when it's not chapter one."

She lives with her daughter on their horse farm in their ancestral hometown of Newfane, New York, minutes from majestic Niagara Falls. Mother and daughter are currently experimenting with scent training their horses for search, rescue, and recovery. Her cast of characters reflect both people she has met while in law enforcement and members of her close-knit community. They are and will continue to be her inspiration to create new storylines and interesting characters.

cellenculverwell.com